About the Authors

Verity and Georgina met at Crackley Hall School at the age of seven. Their long-standing friendship, shared tastes, humour, love of the beautiful Cotswolds and outlook on life has inspired this writing partnership. They are both married and live in leafy Warwickshire with a collection of children and animals between them.

Calamities in Flipping Bodbury

To Val,
Happy Reading!

Love from

Verity x.

Dedications

For my father, John Robert Stew and my husband, Adrian. –*Verity*

For Andrew, Louise and Joseph, with love. – *Georgina*

Georgina Edwards & Verity Stew

Calamities in Flipping Bodbury

A CIP catalogue record for this title is
available from the British Library.

ISBN 978 1 84963 177 8

www.austinmacauley.com

First Published (2012)
Austin & Macauley Publishers Ltd.
25 Canada Square
Canary Wharf
London
E14 5LB

Printed & Bound in Great Britain

Contents

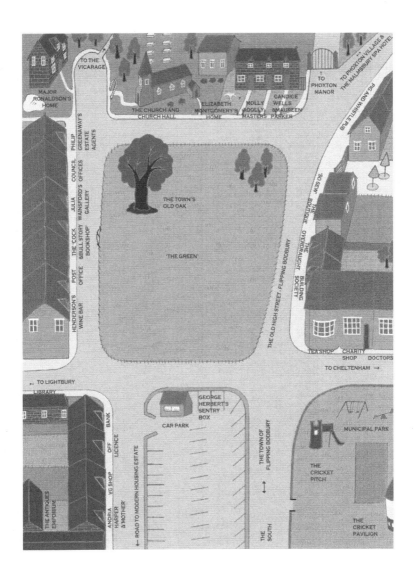

Cast of Characters

HUMANS

Jamie Henderson

Mid-thirties, brought up in the Cotswolds, he joined the Coldstream Guards and served in Afghanistan. Jamie decided to leave the army to pursue a more frivolous life and have some fun. He and his brother opened a wine bar in the town of Flipping Bodbury. Jamie saw several years active service in the army for Queen and Country and is now actively servicing every bored housewife in the vicinity for his own pleasure!

Luke Henderson

Younger brother of Jamie, he was injured in the army and now helps to run Hendersons Wine Bar. His leg was badly affected in a bomb blast. Definitely has the likeability factor.

Phillip Greenaway

Local estate agent and social climber. He is relatively well-educated, but has ideas above his station. Was fairly successful in the late 1990s and lives the typical middle class lifestyle.

Vanessa Greenaway
Phillip's self-absorbed wife who doesn't work and has the ubiquitous two children at private school. Vanessa doesn't join in with anything locally she sees it as beneath her. Attractive in an obvious way, but this doesn't come cheap.

Major Ronaldson
The Major is retired from the Light Infantry, (has no time for Jamie Henderson as he chose to leave the army, but very fond of young Luke who was injured). The Major lives at Belmont Lodge at the bottom of the long drive to Belmont Manor. He has his hopes firmly set on winning over the affections of Elizabeth Montgomery, who is 'of good stock'.

Lila-Belle Ronaldson
Grand-daughter of the Major; a spirited 17 year old girl who attends St Catherine's private girl's school. She is currently studying A Levels when she isn't out partying or at the stables.

Ronnie Webster
Lottery winner, former owner of Belmont Manor. He had to downsize to Hickstead Hall, a smaller modern pad, but still loaded by most people's standards. 'Chav made good'.

Chrissie Webster
Ronnie's wife; blonde beauty therapist who married Ronnie when he won the lottery. She is desperate to be accepted in the town.

Julia Wainsford

A talented local artist. She has a small gallery in the high street in Flipping Bodbury, just along from Hendersons Bar. Mid-forties; attractive, if a bit arty. Julia lives with her trusted Afghan hound, Rufus, and is building a very good life for herself with her painting.

Max Gazeley

The local GP in Phoxton and surrounding area. Max relocated from Harley Street to the Cotswolds having become disillusioned with his superficial clients. Tall, dark and handsome.

Cedric Waterman

Retired Professor of History. He lives in his library, a man of few words who suffers in silence with his eccentric wife. He adores his two daughters.

Winnie Waterman

Wife of Cedric, they live in Fleck Hall, a rambling country house in need of some improvements not unlike Winnie herself. Of ruddy complexion, her looks typify the country stalwart - always in plaid and wool. Winnie is a fantastic fundraiser and champion of the underdog as well as a great cook and a devoted member of the WI.

Jessica Waterman

Daughter of Winnie and Cedric Waterman. Jessica lives and works in Bristol, but makes constant trips home to keep a check on both her parents and help with the crumbling family home.

Bridget Waterman

Youngest daughter of Winnie and Cedric. Bridget was studying Theatre Studies in London when a disastrous affair derailed her. A very attractive and carefree girl.

Patrick Sargeant

Retired Naval Officer, a very close friend of Cedric Waterman's – their mutual interest in naval matters being their established bond. Patrick is a long suffering man who prefers the company of male intellectuals although he adores his bossy wife.

Arlette Sargeant

Wife of Patrick, very committed to the WI – she is the matriarch of the area. Nothing happens locally that Arlette doesn't know about. A very social person, she constantly entertains and organises people – this drives her husband mad.

Anita Carmichael

Niece of Patrick and Arlette Sargeant. A reasonably successful model and bit part actress who aspires to greater things. A real diva.

Alasdair Crossley

Mid-thirties, tall dark and handsome. He runs the family hotel business with help from his sister Miranda. The small hotel chain is known as Crossley Hotels.

Miranda Crossley

Alasdair's sister; a mouse. Not typically pretty but a very

good catch. She is married to her job – she oversees the day to day running of the family hotels. She lives in a flat within The Malmsbury Spa Hotel on the outskirts of the village of Phoxton.

Olivia Beckwith
Events organiser for Crossley Hotels. Often described as shy and dependable. Olivia was at school with Miranda.

Rodney Falstaff
Narcoleptic dentist who was recently forced to take early retirement.

Anoria Harper
Anoria lives with her elderly mother, Winifred. Anoria used to work in the accounts department of 'Bridges and Phocket Department Store' in Cheltenham before her mother's illness meant she had to give up work and become a full time carer. She is a WI member, largely to have a social outlet.

George Herbert
(Of the flat cap brigade) A retired former municipal car park attendant. A stickler for rules and a great upholder of the law. George now runs the Neighbourhood Watch Group on the council estate at the edge of Phoxton.

Warwick Portillo
Former conservative councillor; now a local magistrate. A straight talking individual devoted to the area. Warwick is married to the ravishing Francine.

Marjorie Lloyd-Manning

Marjorie lives at Phoxton Manor with her husband Truman. A keen gardener, she enters all the local competitions and takes them very seriously.

Truman Lloyd-Manning

A retired solicitor and hen-pecked husband to Marjorie. He undertakes many local worthy causes and is committed to upholding the Town's reputation and traditions.

Portia Lloyd-Manning

Marjorie and Truman's niece who is frequently dumped on them because her parents are charity workers. They travel the world but lack responsibility towards their daughter.

Elizabeth Montgomery

Elizabeth is the Lady Chair Person of the Women's Institute. A great fundraiser, organiser and busy body. A stickler for procedure and always to be seen with a clipboard in hand. She is cautiously beginning a romance with Major Ronaldson although she vigorously denies it.

Joan Sidewell

A member of the WI who always gets the main part in their theatrical productions as she had a bit part in Emmerdale some years ago.

Maud Beechy

A widower, member of the WI, a real worrier who panics about everything she is asked to do.

Theodore Bartlett
Theodore had links with minor productions at the RSC in the past and never lets anyone forget this. A retired civil servant.

Nancy Clayton
A younger member of the WI who is always cast in good roles in productions due to her ability to actually remember her lines.

Molly and Dolly Masters
Spinster sisters who run 'SO SEW' sewing shop in town.

Crispin Granger
Tree hugger

Blair and Drew Bantham
The resident gays who own the second hand bookshop in Flipping Bodbury, 'The Cock and Bull Story.'

Maureen Parker
Maureen is tall and thick set and usually found in dungarees, very practical. Her partner is Candice Wells.

Candice Wells
The petite and pretty early 50s partner of Maureen Parker. A thoroughly good person.

Tristram Hackett
Tristram lives at 500 Acre Farm. He is the local laird who still allows his private land to be used for fox hunting. A staunch supporter of the Countryside Alliance.

Mrs Bagworth
Known as 'Old Baggy', who is the cleaning lady to the Lloyd-Mannings, Elizabeth Montgomery and Major Ronaldson. She is a constant source of village gossip.

Keiran Sadler
The local vet who really takes an interest in the community.

Ray Wilcox
Gardener to the Lloyd-Mannings and several other residents of Phoxton. Ray is on the look-out for a wife at the ripe old age of 70 and had harboured high hopes of Elizabeth Montgomery until the Major stepped in.

Mervyn Harper
Known as Merv the Perv for his roving hands. The Liberal Democrat Councillor for the area.

Sheila Harper
Mervyn's social climbing wife who likes to spend his money.

The Reverend Hopeswell
Vicar for the parish of Flipping Bodbury and surrounding villages.

Pippa Hamilton
Pippa runs the local Pony Club branch. Rather chunky and buxom but pretty she is in her early 30s and still lives at home running her parents stables on the outskirts of Flipping Bodbury.

Angus Smythe
The Head of the PE Department at Chartwell Hall; very unpopular and known as 'Angry Angus'.

Guy Picard
Guy is the Fencing Instructor at Chartwell Hall, he is popular with the students and the ladies love him.

ANIMALS

Bounder
The Waterman's Black Labrador; Bounder by name and bounder by nature. A real crotch sniffer. Ideally he should be castrated.

Peggy
The Waterman's Fox Terrier, a spirited little dog with a great sense of duty to the family.

Malvolio
The Lloyd-Manning's naughty male donkey, a trouble maker but a loveable rogue.

Matilda
A brood mare donkey.

Phoxton
The foal of Malvolio and Matilda. Named after the village where she was born.

Cherry and Merry
Two of the donkeys who were dumped at Phoxton Manor.

Willow and Larkin
Elizabeth Montgomery's Siamese cats. Her babies!

The fictitious villages in the Cotswolds area for the purpose of these stories are:

The villages of Phoxton, Lightbury, Chalworth and Modbury together with the town of Flipping Bodbury.

St Catherine's School – for Girls.

Chartwell Hall Public School – for Boys.

The Flipping Bodbury Gazette – The local rag – font of all mis-information.

The Overdraught – A cellar based bistro renowned for its expensive cuisine, but its name derives from its pre-conversion damp and draughty state.

The Pig and Whistle Pub – Youngsters pub in Flipping Bodbury.

The Fox and Hounds Pub – On the edge of Phoxton village by Phoxton Bridge; the ideal spot to view the hunt.

Hendersons Wine Bar – The glory (watering) hole of all the locals.

Donkey Dumping

The exquisite beauty of the valley that stretched out below Marjorie Lloyd-Manning's Cotswold idyll never failed to uplift her. As she drew back the curtains in the sitting room on a crisp autumn morning to admire the view from the French doors, she gave a shriek of horror at the sight that befell her eyes.

"Truman!" Marjorie bellowed at the top of her voice, "Come quickly!"

Truman Lloyd-Manning was enjoying a rare lie-in, and was unwilling to be roused from his slumber and fantasy of being rescued by Joanna Lumley as the latest of her causes to be saved.

"If it's that bloody stream flooding again I shall be straight on to the council," he chuntered, as he pulled on a paisley silk dressing gown and leather slippers. "Tipping leaves into the stream clogging up everything, people can't be bothered to tidy up these days..." It continued as he descended the stairs to find the hysterical Marjorie.

"I don't believe it; look at my herbaceous borders, filthy beasts trampling over my garden. Get out! Get out!" Marjorie shouted as she was banging on the glass.

Joining her at the window, Truman looked upon the usually perfect, manicured garden stretching down to the stream. There upon the lawn, in the borders and trampling everywhere were four tatty donkeys.

"Well I never," gasped Truman, which irritated Marjorie no end because she was expecting something a little more helpful.

"Truman, never mind gawping, do something. Go out there and shoo them away before they eat every last plant."

"How am I supposed to shoo away a quad of donkeys, dear? Where are they supposed to go? I'll have to call the fire brigade." And with that he wandered off to the phone leaving Marjorie still banging on the glass.

Marjorie and Truman Lloyd-Manning lived in Phoxton Manor, in the village of Phoxton, on the edge of the town of Flipping Bodbury. The house was built on a mound which enabled wonderful views of the town and the valley stretching away towards Cheltenham in the far distance. It was a beautiful yellow stone building with wrought iron gates, through which the winding driveway dissected immaculate gardens, which were open to the public each spring. These were largely the work of Marjorie and her trusted gardener, Wilcox, who had suffered Marjorie's exacting demands for years but purely in the horticultural sense.

Truman, having had no luck with the fire brigade, had contacted the RSPCA, only to be told that they would send someone out to have a look at the donkeys as soon as they could. This left the donkeys roaming around the garden without a care in the world, and Marjorie complaining that she could feel one of her migraines coming on.

Arriving later that morning amidst the chaos was Portia Lloyd-Manning, Marjorie and Truman's niece. A fifteen year old teenage girl, who could be either a delight to be with or, terribly sullen depending on her mood that day. She was due to be staying with Marjorie and Truman whilst her parents went off to Haiti. As Red Cross workers their commitment to worthy causes was beyond compare, but less could be said of their commitment to their daughter, who Marjorie believed would also benefit from a little TLC. Marjorie took one of her little pink wonder pills and went to lie down, whilst Truman and Wilcox hastily erected an area behind the house where the donkeys would do less damage, and they could begin the task of repairing the flowerbeds. It was just as they were endeavouring to round up the marauding beasts that Portia arrived by taxi.

"Hello Uncle Tru," she called as she sprawled out of the taxi, "what lovely donkeys."

"Your aunt doesn't think so. Got up this morning to find they'd been dumped here. Marjorie's lying down; she's got one of her heads. Be a dear and give us a hand to round them up." Truman was relieved by her arrival because Portia belonged to the Pony Club and was an excellent rider; he presumed therefore donkeys would be no problem for her.

Some considerable time later, having enticed the donkeys into their newly penned off area with a good deal of bribery in the form of carrots and sugar lumps. Portia had already spotted the ring leader of the four and called him Malvolio. A very timid mare worried Portia the most, together with the fact that all four of the donkeys were persistently coughing. She had just persuaded Truman to call out the local vet when an RSPCA van came up the driveway.

"Fantastic, this could be our salvation and we might actually get Marjorie up in time for dinner if they take this lot away." Truman strode off to get the RSPCA man.

This was not to be the case. Having taken a cursory look over the motley crew, the man from the RSPCA informed Truman they could not be moved to a sanctuary because they had, in his opinion, equine flu and this was probably the reason they had been abandoned in the first place. He suggested calling in Kieran Sadler, the local vet, in order to begin treatment, but he warned it would be costly.

Kieran shortly confirmed the diagnosis – equine flu – and immediately began injecting the donkeys. Portia, who had been worried she would be bored to death at her uncle and aunt's for the holidays, was proving to be a great asset as veterinary nurse and was soon proficient with taking temperatures and checking the donkeys. Kieran also confirmed that the donkeys would need to stay in their temporary accommodation until they were no longer contagious. Whilst Wilcox was despatched to remove the cars from the double garage which would become their temporary shelter, Portia rang to order straw and supplies. Truman went to impart the dreadful news to Marjorie.

"I just want to look at the mare with the crooked ear again." Kieran said to Portia. "Something tells me there might be more than flu troubling her." Kieran carefully examined the timid mare who Portia had named Matilda. "I thought so." He turned to Portia, "She's in foal, we'll have to be extra vigilant with her, equine flu could cause her to go into an early labour." He noticed Portia's worried face, "I'll call back tomorrow and see how they're all doing. Watch what Matilda eats and make sure she has plenty to drink." Malvolio had kept up a constant nudging of Kieran whilst he had been examining Matilda.

"I think we have an anxious father-to-be here," he laughed as Portia received a more forceful bump whilst trying to tether Matilda.

The cup of tea rattled in the saucer as Truman entered the darkened bedroom some time later to face his wife. She lay groaning in the darkness and Truman prepared himself.

"Well my dear, the good news is that the donkeys are all safely in an enclosure now and Wilcox is repairing the damage." He spoke quietly so as not to add to her pain.

"What's the bad news then?" Marjorie was not one to be fooled easily.

"I was just coming to that. It seems we may have our visitors for a little while longer, they have flu, and one is in foal so she can't be moved just now." Truman prepared himself for a wail.

"Oh no!!!" Marjorie pulled the covers over her head and was not seen again that day.

Portia was in her element. She spent the next couple of days looking after the donkeys, feeding them their medication, cleaning out the garage and removing the boisterous donkeys out of the way so that Matilda could remain quietly resting. Visitors were arriving by the bus load as news spread around that donkey dumping had taken place on the hallowed ground of Phoxton Manor. On Thursday afternoon however, when Portia went to check on the group, Malvolio was nowhere to be seen and she realised that the temporary enclosure was open at one corner.

Malvolio had had a tremendous day; initially he had merely rubbed against the corner of the enclosure to rid himself of an itch, but the movement had loosened the bindings and he had gently nudged the metal stands apart and wandered off down the drive. His first port of call had been the church of St Nicholas on the edge of Phoxton village. Having trampled over a couple of freshly filled graves and discovered he didn't like the taste of chrysanthemums, he turned his attention to the open church doorway and followed the scent of apples. The Church, having recently held a harvest festival service, was still decked out with arrangements of fruit. It had been decided that this produce should not be distributed to the local elderly for fear that too much fibre might have unpleasant effects on their constitutions.

Exiting Hendersons, Winnie Waterman tripped over.

"Whoops; that step wasn't there when we arrived." Laughing she linked arms with the gorgeous Drew.

Arlette followed helping Blair, Drew's partner and

co-owner of the local bookstore, into his large Astrakhan coat. They had attended a meeting of the local WI and transferred from the drafty church hall to the cosiness of the wine bar to continue making plans for the next fundraising project, a sponsored pole dance to raise money for a homeless tramp living on the edge of the village. It had been a controversial meeting as many felt the tramp should simply accept the council's generous offer of lodgings, and those who understood his turning it down due to his need to be wandering. The fundraising committee decided to provide a B&Q shed for him for shelter in the winter, adjacent to the local allotments and a year's supply of Meals on Wheels. Drew and Blair were honorary members of the local WI partly because of their incredible cake making skills, and partly because they provided a constant stream of entertainment.

"You look like a drugs baron!" Arlette remarked slipping on the wet path. As they rounded the corner, Winnie spotted the donkey merrily trotting through the church door, dodging gravestones and heading for the main road, where he gaily followed the white line in the centre of the road like a drunk being put through his paces!

"What on earth – quick there will be an accident if we don't do something!" Arms outstretched, the four of them herded him onto the pavement where he proceeded to enter Elizabeth Montgomery's (Lady Chair of the WI) front garden.

"Shoo Shoo!" she shouted, running out of the house in her pink candlewick house coat and brandishing an umbrella. "Get away you beast." She swung the umbrella at Malvolio as he nonchalantly started nuzzling one of the large stone hogs adjacent to the drive.

Hearing the commotion and having watched the marauding group exiting the wine bar, Major Ronaldson who was retired from the Light Infantry and a formidable member of the community, approached from the other side of the green.

"What on earth's the matter?" He headed straight for Elizabeth's side. Resplendent in a paisley smoking jacket and monogrammed navy slippers, he looked like an old movie hero, Elizabeth thought.

"Oh dear Major, I seem to have gained a stray and he's taken rather a shine to my Fritz."

"Who?" Asked the Major.

"Fritz my stone hog – Oh dear I'm feeling rather faint."

"I think a stiff drink is in order my dear," said the Major, ushering her through her front door, and seizing an opportunity he had been waiting for for many years. "Move that damned animal on." He called out to Winnie and Arlette as he entered Marjorie's house, leaving the donkey to his courting of the hog.

"Well at least he's off the road," said Winne with a smile "I'll call Truman and let him know his whereabouts, hand me your belt," she added to Blair. "I'll tie it round him and Fritz, and he'll stay put till Truman gets here."

Reluctantly Blair handed over the belt only after considerable reassurance from Winnie that donkeys don't eat Astrakhan.

"Do let's nip back for a celebration drinkie, it only seems fitting in the circumstances," Blair announced as he turned on his heel heading back to the wine bar, closely followed by the others.

"On the third day she rose again," Truman muttered under his breath as Marjorie wandered into the kitchen on Thursday evening.

"I thought I would try and get up for a while." She remarked weakly and with a hand pressed to her forehead.

"Good show my dear, sit down while I make you a nice cup of tea." Truman, anxious not to allow his wife to have a relapse and force him to continue fending for himself and Portia, pulled out a chair and aided her descent.

As the phone rang in the hallway Truman dashed off to answer it before the noise sent Marjorie's migraine soaring again. Portia had alerted everyone she could think of about the disappearance of the naughty animal, and Mr Wilcox was driving round the lanes looking for him but so far to no avail. Returning to the kitchen, Truman signalled to Portia that Malvolio had been found; he made his excuses to Marjorie and headed out to retrieve him.

By the time Truman had located Malvolio he had eaten through the Astrakhan lead and was merrily munching on the "Phoxton in Bloom" pansy displays on the Green. Portia having ensured that her aunt was safely soaking in a warm bath, headed out after Truman with a rope and makeshift collar to catch the wayward donkey. She arrived at the Green just in time to see Truman, the Major and Elizabeth both in a state of undress pulling and pushing at the donkey to remove him from the pansies, and were trying to entice him with yet more food. Malvolio who had consumed far too many apples in the church earlier, was now swaying unsteadily and dumped a steaming load of manure at their feet. This was all too much for the Lady Chair of the WI, who with a shriek retreated to the arms of the Major who ushered her safely back in doors.

Having done their best to repair the pansy displays Portia and Truman slowly walked a slightly drunk Malvolio back to Phoxton Manor where they found that Matilda had gone into labour. To Portia's amazement Marjorie was kneeling beside the distressed donkey rubbing her back and urging her on. Truman was despatched to call Kieran the vet but returned with the news that he was already out at the nearby stud where a prize flat race mare was foaling. He assured Truman that he would contact a locum to help them and also suggested that they seek help from Tristram Hackett, a local cattle farmer, who may lend them a hand, as he had a great deal of experience of delivering calves.

Marjorie switched into midwife mode despite her silk pyjamas and robe, and ordered Portia to find blankets and water and to remove the other donkeys to the far side of the garage. Matilda, whickering and clearly distressed, was struggling and failing to get to her feet. Portia and Marjorie remained in place with Matilda throughout the night, and when Truman informed them that Tristram was away at a Country

Show they simply knuckled down to the task ahead. Truman sat on a bale of hay, and having Googled how to deliver a foal, he managed to find an online website with a vet working the night shift who was able to keep them on track and supply advice to the makeshift midwifes. Portia had fetched a whining Malvolio and tied him near to Matilda; this appeared to comfort the pregnant donkey and her whickering began to subside. As the first sign of daylight broke, Matilda with the help of Truman and Marjorie were by now covered in straw and sweat, struggled to her feet in order to give one final effort and deliver the foal. The front legs and head appeared first, and as instructed by the online vet, Marjorie gently stepped forward and began to pull the rest of the foal from a tiring Matilda, who due to her illness was unable to summon the necessary energy to push anymore. Marjorie, covered in slime and blood, and exhausted looked triumphant as the foal slid to the ground. She hastily encouraged Matilda to lick the foal and ensure the bond between them was secured, as Kieran screeched up the drive.

"Well, well," he called out upon entering the garage, "we have a new midwife in our midst." He looked at Marjorie in her unusually dishevelled state and she beamed back at him. Immediately he began to check over the little foal as Marjorie was hugged by a tearful Portia and very proud Truman.

"This little girl needs a name," remarked Kieran after assuring them that she was well, if a little feeble and in need of rest and care which he felt sure they would provide but otherwise likely to be a fine addition to the group.

"We're going to call her Phoxton," replied Portia, looking at her aunt who nodded her approval.

Marjorie's maternal instincts well and truly took over. She was very taken with little Phoxton to the point where she was sneaking out at night to check on her and Portia, who insisted in keeping an all-night vigil by lying in a sleeping bag lying next to them in the straw. Rather than adopting her more natural stance of worrying about Portia catching a cold and remonstrating with her, she fetched her extra blankets, hot water bottles and a thermos of hot chocolate and kept a constant supply of warmed oats for Matilda and Phoxton, even allowing the other donkeys onto the back lawn to graze and recuperate.

Soon Phoxton was gaining strength and weight and trotting about outside, and Marjorie had to consider that there was little reason now for the donkeys to remain at Phoxton Manor. With her heart feeling a growing sense of ownership, but her head knowing that there was no permanent space for the donkeys to remain in situ, Marjorie assumed the role of donkey champion and began to undertake the challenge of albeit with a heavy heart.

An emergency meeting of the WI was called with the sole aim of finding a place for the donkeys to remain within the community. Marjorie, determined to keep them altogether, had her work cut out in convincing Elizabeth Montgomery, who was still smarting over Malvolio getting amorous with her hog. However, this incident had led to her and Major Ronaldson spending a good deal of time together and for that reason alone she was willing to add her considerable weight to the project. Winnie Waterman and Arlette Sargeant, two wayward members of the WI, had taken a real shine to Malvolio during his adventure in the churchyard, so were committed to fighting to keep the donkeys nearby. Over the next week the donkeys and their plight occupied much conversation in the town.

The local nursery visited the donkeys and Portia helped them feed Phoxton warmed oats. The infant school brought donations of carrots and other vegetables to help feed them, and the WI ladies arrived in their droves with knitted blankets, which should have been sent to the homeless in Cheltenham, but everyone had agreed that charity should begin nearer to home. The story of the rescue of the donkeys was even spreading to the local newspaper and radio station. Brown Owl had seized upon the opportunity to involve the local brownie pack who had been coming to help Portia muck out the garage/stable as part of their pet care and animal rescue badges. Marjorie, now in her element as her notoriety spread, was being hailed as a true benefactor of these poor creatures, and she had conveniently forgotten her initial horror at their arrival.

Just as it seemed that the donkeys were to become a permanent fixture at Phoxton Manor, the RSPCA Inspector returned to say he had secured sanctuary for them in Devon and would be sending transportation to collect them the following day. Marjorie's heart sank at the thought of them being taken so far away, and was astounded to hear herself inform the gentleman that she would be keeping the animals herself.

"I don't know if you are quite aware Mrs Lloyd-Manning that there are certain regulations and requirements that need to be complied with before I can pass this dwelling as fit for a donkey sanctuary." The RSPCA man looked uncomfortable as he imparted this news.

"My good man," Marjorie retorted, "I am entirely aware of the requirements of these animals and am in the process of securing a large paddock to the rear of my property where I shall erect magnificent dwellings for these beasts." With that she snatched the paperwork from the RSPCA man and proceeded to walk him back to his vehicle.

"I will be back in three weeks to inspect the facilities, but I've got to say I really admire your spirit." He smiled at her as he got into his van and headed off down the drive.

Marjorie turned to Truman nervously,

"Can we buy the paddock that old Jones is selling?" she asked timidly.

"Is there any point in my saying no, my dear?" Truman replied, exasperated.

All Things Occult

"The Cock and Bull Story" second-hand bookshop was a hive of activity for a normally quiet Thursday morning. Preparations were underway for a book signing, a new departure for Drew and Blair Bantham. The town was beginning to show signs of Halloween Fever – this being the end of October, merchandise was available in all the shops, and pumpkins of varying sizes were cropping up on the pavements.

Drew Bantham, one half of Drew and Blair, the bookshop owners had been compiling lists of jobs still to do, whilst Blair was busily fussing over piles of books to be signed and lining up biros to ensure a plentiful supply.

"I don't know whether to ere on the side of caution and only put out a few copies or go for broke and expect a throng." Blair turned to Drew his concern apparent on his face.

"Stop worrying; there'll be plenty of people turn up. There's nothing this town likes more than a good gawp, they'll be out in droves." Drew tried to reassure him.

"I hope you're right Drew Bantham, poor Anoria's in such a flap. I told her, 'don't you think JK suffered these kind of nerves when little Harry P was merely a twinkle in her eye.'" Blair swept his hand across his forehead in mock desperation and piled more copies of "All Things Occult" on the green leather inlay.

Anoria Harper, the author of "All Things Occult" was indeed in a flap. She had selected her favourite cardigan and slacks for the book signing and was desperately organising 'mother', who could be a cantankerous old bat at the best of times. This had taken a good deal of forethought as 'mother' liked her meals at certain times, and insisted on Anoria being present whilst she watched Emmerdale, despite the fact that it wasn't about farming like in the old days, her constant refrain. Mrs Hubbard from Spruce Cottage had agreed to pop in and sit with mother whilst Anoria snuck out to the signing. She knew nothing about Anoria's foray into the literary world and Anoria intended to keep it that way.

The true blurb on the book back cover would read that Anoria Harper, spinster, member of the WI had formerly worked in the accounts department of 'Bridges and Phocket' Department Store in Cheltenham. This was before being forced to leave her beloved job in order to become a full-time carer for her elderly incapacitated mother, Winifred, but simply known as 'mother' to all and sundry. Unbeknown to the locals and her fellow WI members, Anoria had been fascinated by the occult since her early teens when she had become accidentally involved in a religious cult. (Accidentally - because Anoria thought she was filling in an application to work for a local vicar and his family, when in actual fact she was answering an advertisement in the paper for girls who had an interest in 'running a household and servicing the Yodall Sect'. Anoria, largely to spite her domineering mother, had gone to North Yorkshire to give it a go anyway. The weird religious practices hadn't fazed her but merely opened her eyes to a whole new world beyond her cosy Cotswold upbringing, nor had the communal living dented her enthusiasm, after all, she'd had no privacy at home with an interfering 'mother'. No, what finally sent Anoria packing back to the Cotswolds was when the sect entered into a month of fasting, and at that point Anoria thought enough was enough and headed home to her mother's jam roly poly and never looked back. However, the interlude had laid the seed of interest in other forms of religious worship, and whilst Anoria spent the next few years diligently balancing the accounts at 'Bridges and Phocket', she was also reading all she could find on the occult.

Drew and Blair admired Anoria enormously, it took a great deal of patience to put up with her mother, and they knew only too well what it was like to be different from the mainstream. Any free time Anoria did get was either spent in the bookshop with the boys or helping out at the WI. When Anoria finally admitted to them she had been compiling a book, they made it their mission to guide her forward into the literary world. As posters went up around the town and invitations were sent out to VIPs, the buzz and gossip was immense. The locals had Anoria pegged as a lonely spinster who lived the most sheltered of lives, and therefore the Bantham's knew that the turnout for this event would be huge if only for the because of the shock factor.

Staring through the orange and black festooned window of the book store, Drew commented on the efforts of the other shopkeepers.

"Nice to see everyone's entered into the spirit of things, so to speak."

Heaps of autumnal leaves were scattered as a backdrop for Halloween scenes, Witches' brooms, cobwebs and rubber rats were just some of the props used by the locals to dress their establishments for the spookiest day of the year, and hopefully to cash in by adding Halloween touches to everything they sold. 'The Overdraught', the local bistro was offering a set meal including the obligatory pumpkin soup starter and Goulash!! Even the Post Office had decorated its window with orange and black A4 ring binders, notepads and other themed stationery.

"I am truly amazed Blair, by how enterprising everyone's been; it's really quite refreshing." He ran a duster over the skirting whilst trying not to disturb the fake cobwebs.

By early evening it was suitably dark and guests were starting to arrive, the first being Chrissie and Ronnie Webster, who could be seen crossing the road. Ronnie in a pinstripe suit, hair in 'toute direction' sprayed white, big black rings round his eyes; and Chrissie in the tightest corset, sporting a very tall black hat, long black wig and large spider necklace that nestled happily amongst her best assets that were most definitely on show tonight (no doubt in honour of the Henderson brothers, who were hosting the after-signing lock in).

"Marvellous, marvellous, Ronnie, you must be Michael Keaton from 'Beetlejuice', and Chrissie, well I'm speechless'." Handing them drinks, he busied himself filling the tray with a Pernod concoction to serve to the stream of people arriving early. The locals really had turned out in force: Jamie & Luke, dressed as Dead Butlers, Arlette & Patrick as the Corpse Bride & Groom, Jessica & Bridget, Willo the wisps, Julia Wainsford as the white lady and Phillip and Vanessa Greenaway (coaxed on the proviso that she could book herself in for a spa day!) Always working, Phillip was hoping that if the book were a success, Anoria might be in need a more palatial pad. The guests mingled, haphazardly leafing through the selection on offer, but Anoria's book caused the greatest stir and appeared to be flying off the shelves on this most bewitching of nights.

Tapping his glass, Blair asked for quiet.

"Ladies and Gentleman, I would like to thank you all for making this book signing a great success. Anoria is indeed a dark horse, none of us here until recently were aware of her aptitude for 'All things Occult', but we are proud to be the first bookshop to promote this most controversial of literary tastes, made extra special by the illustrations of our very own local artist, the wonderfully talented, Julia Wainsford. It just remains for me to declare this signing officially open, and I would ask that you form an orderly queue, Drew will be happy to assist you with your purchases, so over to you Anoria." And with that he raised his glass to loud cheers.

The evening passed in a daze of glory and Anoria soaked up both the interest in her book, and the stream of glasses of Devil's punch that were put before her. The novelty of being the centre of attention meant she maintained her flushed cheeks all evening, and even though many were merely there for the free booze and pumpkin nibbles on offer, Anoria was blissfully unaware of any such intention.

As the last purchase passed through the till, the guests started making their way to Hendersons, in search of more drink and revelry. Inside the staff had gone to town, Jack o' Lanterns and candles added to the eerie décor and in true Henderson style the buffet reflected the occasion. Above the bar, black bulbs replaced the usual lighting, showing up everyone's white underwear, and more unfortunately for Ronnie, who was first in the queue, all his capped teeth; Julia, Jamie and Luke were almost uncontrollable.

"This is like a testament to the work of Rodney Falstaff; what a shame he's not here to see his own handiwork!" They all fell about, "He's no doubt tucked up in bed fast asleep." Julia giggled through her drink induced euphoria.

As the last staff member left, Luke locked the doors.

"I've set us a table in the snug for the séance, hope everyone's still up for it." Glances were exchanged. Anoria now five sheets to the wind, was first to take her seat.

"Let's get started." She said, with a new found confidence. At least she definitely knew more than the assembled company. Ronnie sat between Julia and Chrissie, with Luke and Jamie either side of Anoria and Jess, Bridget, Drew and Blair, and the Greenaways with their backs to the window.

The large round table had a glass in the middle and numbers and letters set out in a circle, the large church candles placed on the window sills gave just enough light to observe any messages.

"I'll make notes," Jessica offered.

"That would be very helpful Jessica, but I thought we'd try table tilting first. It is one of the oldest forms of spiritual contact you know." Anoria closed her eyes. "Right everyone, place your hands on the table with little fingers touching." She took a deep breath, head back. "Is there anybody there?" Anoria's voice rang out, "Is there anybody there?"

There was much nudging and giggling as nerves and alcohol were getting the better of everyone.

"I don't think I like this." Chrissie wailed. "It's scaring me." She hiccupped.

"Ssh, be serious." Blair closed his eyes. "I've been told I have the gift, let me try. Come forward spirits," he called in a dramatic voice. "Come forward, we don't wish to hurt you. Do you wish to communicate with anyone here assembled?"

The others giggled.

"Did you feel that?" Blair's voice rose hysterically. "The table definitely moved!" he squealed.

"You're over reacting. They won't come if you take the mickey." Anoria took over. "If you are here knock once for yes, twice for no."

Julia giggled. "Well they're hardly going to knock twice if they're not here are they," she laughed.

Only Anoria, Drew and Blair appeared to be taking things seriously, the others were too far gone to behave sensibly, but they continued nonetheless.

"Ssh, there's definitely something happening." A snoring noise could be heard.

"Ronnie wake up you'll miss the best bit." Chrissie nudged him and Ronnie woke with a start and a snort, not quite sure where he was. At that the table appeared to start vibrating slightly.

"Oh my God, there is someone here," Blair whispered. At that a light tapping could be heard on the window, and peering through the gloom Blair could make out a shadowy white figure, with long white hair, moaning, face pressed up against the glass; he screamed like a girl.

"Oh my God it's the white lady!" Jumping onto Drew's knee he hid his face.

"Who is that?" The Henderson brothers leapt up from their seats and headed towards the door.

"I told you it was real. I have the gift." Anoria seemed elated that this apparition had given weight to her first publication, whilst everyone else had turned whiter than the visiting spectre.

"It's a ghost, it's a ghost!" Chrissie screamed and passed out.

"Hold on a minute." Luke moved closer to the

window and parted the curtains more fully with his walking stick.

Recognition dawned as Blair whimpered, "Err Anoria, I think your mother's here."

"She can't be," Anoria replied giggling still heavily under the influence of the devil's brew, "she's not dead yet."

Opening the stable door, letting in a blast of icy cold wind, Winifred appeared. She let out a blood curdling shriek as Luke's costume scared the remaining life out of her and had to be steadied by Drew and Blair.

"Anoria, Anoria, is my Anoria with you? I've been looking for her everywhere. I just took a look outside and locked myself out. Old Mother Hubbard's drunk all the sherry and is snoring in the lounge. I can't get back in."

"Coming Mother," Anoria sighed with resignation and disappointment. She stood up to leave.

"What on earth is going on here? And why are you out so late, I've had to tape Emmerdale, this really isn't on." Winifred pulled her nightclothes around her and adjusted her glasses as she took in the sight before her.

"As you're here and you must be very cold, let's have a little night cap to warm you up, Mrs H." Luke's charm was too much even for Winifred to resist

"Oh well just a small one, it is quite chilly out." She seated herself at the table, and to the shock of the assembled group announced with a smile.

"Now if you wanted a séance you should have

invited a professional. Move over Anoria, mother knows best." She took up her place and everyone linked hands again, looking astonished at Winifred.

"Well where do you think she got her gift from?" She remarked as she settled into a slow head roll.

The witching hour came and went, and the next morning everyone woke feeling a little worse for wear; Chrissie woke feeling ghastly, her heavy black make-up now transferred to the pillowcase and one false eyelash stuck to Ronnie's back. Arlette and Patrick never made it past the drawing room; Jamie and Luke were found by the cleaner asleep on the floor of the snug.

In the chintzy flat above the bookshop Drew, turning over in bed, stretched and opened his eyes.

"Morning Anoria, Morning Mother... ANORIA, MOTHER!!" and united in shock and embarrassment, they all four sat up in bed.

"Anyone for tea?" Drew's voice trailed off.

Bonfire Delight

The residents of Flipping Bodbury and neighbouring villages had turned out in force on a cold, clear November 5th evening. The town council had, after much consideration, agreed that the annual bonfire event could be held on the land adjacent to the cricket pitch, which had caused consternation amongst the cricket committee who, despite the need of a new pavilion, were not quite ready for the current one to go up in flames. Anyone who was anyone, or who thought they were, was standing about waiting for the great pile to be set alight. Major Ronaldson, head of the committee for town social events had organised a pig roast, and refreshments were hastily being consumed due to the freezing temperatures and delay in starting. Despite the cold, the weather had been kind to the event this year with no sign of rain; the clear skies would allow the fireworks to be seen at their best. The recession having hit even the cash rich residents of Flipping Bodbury (no down at heel council estates exist in this southerly corner of the Cotswolds) had meant that donations for fireworks were somewhat meagre, and therefore much was being made of the bonfire itself and free beverages. Major Ronaldson, a force to be reckoned with when on a crusade, had managed to persuade Ronnie Webster and his wife Chrissie to provide the lion's share of the funding for the evening. Ronnie Webster, a lottery winner who had recently downsized from Belmont Manor to Hickstead Hall (even lottery winners are affected by the recession!) was desperate to be considered part of the south Cotswold elite rather than chav made good, and was only too willing to be exploited in this way. Ronnie's wife Chrissie had been trying to join the WI for several weeks, the matriarchs of which had been steadfastly determined to exclude this new moneyed addition and so Chrissie religiously attended every public event possible in order to curry favour with the leading ladies of Flipping Bodbury.

One such WI aficionado was Winnie Waterman, who was running a toffee apple stall in aid of blind dogs as opposed to guide dogs for the blind. Always one to back the underdog, she felt more affinity with this particular cause than the more mainstream one. Aided and abetted as always by her partner in crime, Arlette Sargeant, who had no special affinity with charity but loved a good knees up! Winnie's daughter, Jessica, home for a visit from Bristol, always keen to get back to her beloved Cotswolds, was busily organising the first aid tent which would inevitably be put to good use when the children were handed the sparklers. Health and safety directives had not yet reached this cosseted part of England and therefore such horrendously dangerous past-times were still permitted.

The honour of setting light to the wood pile this year had been given to Julia Wainsford, not exactly a celebrity in the style of Cheryl Cole; however, she had recently had a small review of her latest water colour exhibitions in The Flipping Bodbury Gazette, and therefore was considered to be a worthy recipient of this prestigious accolade. Julia, who's actual age was mid-forties, though she looked considerably less, was a good looking woman, single and self-sufficient and on the hit list for many of the ardent males in the area. She prided herself on having had a boob job with her first commission cheque from a wealthy horse-owner who had the hots for her, and she was a strong advocate of Pilates which she felt kept her supple and bendy! Approaching the pile with safety matches and a bottle of petrol with a rag protruding from its neck (again health and safety not featuring highly in this neck of the woods) she looked at the unusual specimen which she gathered was Flipping Bodbury's idea of a guy. It resembled more a new age hippie casually reclining whilst supposedly defending a nuclear bomb site. Under pressure to make a formal speech, she simply managed:

"I declare this bonfire lit." Giggling with embarrassment, she struck the match, and hurled the petrol forward into the pile, whereupon a loud explosion ricocheted around the crowd and the pile was well and truly on fire.

"Good work Julia," shouted Jamie Henderson, stepping forward and taking the matches from her trembling hands, "there's nothing like getting things off with a bang."

"Stop taking the mickey, Jamie," Major Ronaldson interrupted, "Miss Wainsford could've been seriously injured."

"No harm done, and at least she got everyone's attention," laughed Luke, Jamie's younger brother.

Julia, now seeing the funny side, began to giggle too. The attention of the Henderson brothers was worth a bit of scorched arm hair by anyone's reckoning. The brothers ran Hendersons Wine Bar in Flipping Bodbury, dashing young ex-army servicemen, they were never short of female attention, and it was their looks and charm that kept the wine bar consistently stocked with the lusty women of the villages and their husbands who were mainly there to keep an eye on them.

"You need a stiff one, Miss Wainsford." Jamie grinned at her, "and we need a drink too!" Luke nearly choked on his pork and stuffing batch but fortunately the Major didn't hear as he had already marched off to chastise a bunch of youths who were happily sword fighting with sparklers.

Julia Wainsford's life to date had not been an easy one. The middle child always struggling for attention, she had blossomed late and found art college to be her salvation from a middle class up-bringing. Julia's parents believed that entering the civil service was the only way to get on in life legitimately. Quite by accident she had met her husband whilst on a painting holiday in Corfu, and her unexpected pregnancy had forced her to give up any hope of pursuing a career in art and instead she became a housewife and mother. Duncan, the said husband, had after 18 years of marriage, come home one day and announced that after much soul searching he had decided to become Veronica. After the initial shock Julia, having experienced the annoyance of having a younger sister who constantly borrowed her clothes and makeup without asking, felt that, frankly having already been there once she was not about to go there again. Julia also felt that despite her husband's need for a change of sexuality, she actually was rather fond of his dangly bits and therefore she was reluctant to accept one without the other. So Duncan, now Veronica, promptly took himself off to New Zealand where he felt he might better adjust to his new persona, and the children of the marriage, twins Luke and Polly, left home shortly after to pursue further education and large student loans. Julia had moved to the Cotswolds, and slowly picked up her creativity again and began producing water colours inspired by her beautiful surroundings. She had not been short of male attention since her arrival in Flipping Bodbury, but having suffered at the hands (and other parts of the body) of one unscrupulous, philandering male resident she was determined not to make the same mistake again.

Hendersons Wine Bar was heaving by the time Julia and the boys had made their way there through the bonfire crowd, and as they entered she was just beginning to feel uncomfortable in the company of such virile young men when a large whiskey was thrust into her hand. After a couple of gulps she began to relax. The less than beautiful people of the neighbourhood frequented the Pig and Whistle pub on the road out of town towards Phoxton, whilst the glam set resided in Hendersons, drinking Martini cocktails, a resurrection from the 80s when Joan Collins had made them as popular as shoulder pads and skinny leg jeans, also currently seeing a revival.

Julia settled into a booth flanked by Jamie and Luke and marvelled at the attention the boys received from the female clientele, and a good deal of the males. As the sound of the firework crescendo came to a halt the bar began to fill up even more, and each time the door opened a wonderful waft of bonfire smoke drifted into the room. Julia sipped away merrily whilst Jamie and Luke discussed who was in the bar, and she noticeably relaxed into this enviable situation. However, as local estate agent and would-be suitor for Julia, Phillip Greenaway, sauntered in, flushed presumably from the heat of the fire or perhaps as a result of an encounter with a cuckolded husband, she feigned more interest than she felt in the discussion in the hope of avoiding contact with him. Julia had consistently rebuked Phillip's advances partly out of respect for his long suffering wife, and partly because his reputation as a shocking philanderer went before him. Phillip's prowess as an artful lover had recently received a set back as a jilted girlfriend had taken out a full page advert in the Flipping Bodbury Gazette stating amongst other things that despite the fact that this estate agent was very quick to put his sale board up, he was also disappointingly quick to rush from exchange to completion! She wasn't necessarily referring to his conveyancing skills. Phillip had kept a low profile for some time after this mortifying retribution, but was once again hotly pursuing Julia. Glancing over to the table she was at he was distinctly alarmed to see that she was in the company of the Henderson boys.

Having consumed a few too many whiskies under the premise that she was still in shock from her bonfire experience, Julia began to tell the boys the tale of the demise of her husbands' genitalia, her subsequent relocation to the Cotswolds, her disappointing affair with a married man and the unwanted attention of the Phillip the local lothario. It was at this point that the boys vowed to make Julia their cause and find her a decent male with which to brighten up her days. As the evening progressed she became increasingly convinced that this was to be the beginning of a very interesting new chapter in the life of Julia Wainsford.

An Unlucky Rabbit's Foot

It was early afternoon on a cold Friday 24th December, and Jessica waited patiently at the station for the train to Cirencester where she hoped to be met by her mother, Winnie. Thickset, grey haired and in her early sixties, Jessica's mother was an essential and eccentric member of the local WI, but decidedly scatty, and it was more by luck than judgement that she sailed through life oblivious to the undercurrents and complications of life in the 21st century. Winnie remained cocooned from the rest of the world in her beautiful Cotswold village. Clutching her steaming cup of tea Jessica considered whether her mother was likely to remember to collect her, whilst she watched as snow began fall, slowly at first but gathering momentum and bringing with it a feeling of childish expectation.

Stepping down from the train an hour later Jessica was amazed and delighted to see her mother, arms flailing heading towards her.

"Jessie!" her mother called out to her as she hauled her case down from the carriage. "Lovely to see you darling, a bit on the thin side but nothing a few days home-cooking won't fix. Do hurry, I've the Christmas pudding on the stove, everything's underway. I've had my hand up a goose's bum all morning." Winnie strode on ahead of her daughter, barely pausing for breath whilst she relayed all the local gossip.

"Hello mum, lovely to see you too." Jessica called to her mother's departing back, and catching up with her she threw her suitcase into the back of the dilapidated land rover and they were off.

"Seat-belt darling," Winnie prompted her daughter and Jessica immediately lapsed back into being a young girl again, no longer an independent adult in her mother's company. The tired old Land Rover jerked forwards and they headed unsteadily for home. Cosy houses lit with twinkling lights gave a magical feel to the fading late afternoon light; clean, new snow blanketed the ground like icing sugar, and Jessica began to relax and look forward to all the Waterman family Christmas traditions.

"We have an extra visitor for Christmas dinner," her mother announced, as they made their way gingerly along the country lanes already becoming slippery with snow. "Arlette's niece is joining them. Arlette says she's a handful but they're stuck with her unexpectedly and Patrick insists she be made welcome." Jessica sat back and listened to the gossip about Anita Carmichael, Arlette's niece; a model in London and a bit-part actress who according to Arlette thought a lot of herself. She'd suddenly called and asked if she could join them for Christmas as she longed for a complete break in the country and her parents were already being joined by her sister and three children whom she couldn't bear to spend time with. Nodding in all the right places and trying to sound deeply interested in these new arrangements for Christmas, Jessica was somewhat disappointed to have to share precious family time with a stranger.

A ghostly quiet greeted them as they approached the long drive, festive lights in the large yew trees gave a beautiful festive glow and Jessica wondered how her poor father had managed to climb up to hang the lights, but was incredibly grateful that he had because it looked magical. The coach lantern hanging from the Cotswold stone porch lit up the front of the house. Jessica loved coming home, a baronial house of great proportions nestled in the beautiful Cotswold countryside, but definitely becoming a little bit more shabby each time she came home as her parents were getting older and less able to maintain their rambling home. Once inside, Christmas spirit engulfed Jessica as huge banks of holly festooned the old wooden staircase, and a ten foot tree dressed with generations old decorations took her breath away. The scent of pine lingered festively in the air; the anticipation of the season lifted her spirits and brought forth a sense of nostalgia and excitement that reminded her of her childhood. Just as she put her case down in the large square hall to admire the decorations, Winnie opened the door to the kitchen and two frantic dogs hurled themselves at Jessica, closely followed by her father, Cedric who despite being a retired academic, still spent almost his entire existence locked away in his study. However, his eyes shone brightly at the sight of his first born and he whisked her off with the dogs for a long walk and catch up, leaving Winnie to her hors d'oeuvre preparation.

On Christmas Day the Waterman's traditionally held a drinks party. These gatherings were famed for the flowing alcohol, relaxed cosy atmosphere and Winnie Waterman's stodgy but delicious canapés. Jessica mingled, topping up glasses, dodging the probing questions into her love-life and reloading plates of food. As the dogs began to bark again signifying more guests, Jessica opened the front door to Arlette Sargeant shouting orders to her heavily laden husband, Patrick, who was staggering behind her.

"Leave the cases till later Patrick; we don't need them now. Ahh! Jessie, Merry Christmas angel. Do take these. Have you heard about the problems with our waterworks Jessie? Mess everywhere, thank goodness your mother insisted we come here for Christmas." Arlette thrust two wilting poinsettias at her and headed off towards the drawing room in search of the party, leaving Patrick to struggle with the luggage.

"Hello Jessie, Happy Christmas love." Patrick kissed both her cheeks. "This is Anita, our niece, visiting from London." Before Jessica stood a tall, dark haired woman with striking features but no warmth in her eyes. She was wearing a huge fur coat which Jessica very much hoped was imitation and was staring at her mobile.

"Hello," Anita distractedly spoke to Jessica as she dropped her coat onto an already overladen Jessica.

"Be an angel Jess and take Anita in and introduce her, I have brie and salmon in the car to bring in yet."

Patrick disappeared back through the front door, slipping on the snow as he went.

Jessica was just about to take Anita through to the party as Bridget, her younger sister, came into the hallway stamping snow all over the tiles with Bounder and Peggy, the family dogs thundering behind her. Bounder by name and bounder by nature immediately sensing a new arrival rammed his nose straight into Anita's crotch, his normal approach to newcomers.

"Oh, dogs," Anita remarked with a distinct edge to her voice as she tried to back away. "I'm allergic to dogs, could you possibly remove them." She dramatically reached into her Louis Vuitton bag and pulled out a packet of pills. "Antihistamine," she remarked "I'll need you to keep them away from me at all times. I wasn't told you had dogs." Fortunately by way of distraction her mobile rang and she dashed off to a quiet corner to take the call.

Patrick returned once again struggling with bags of presents and a large fresh salmon.

"Arlette left you with all the bags again Patrick?" Bridget winked at him, knowing full well she would already be in the thick of the party.

"I know my place love," Patrick winked at her and headed off to the kitchen.

The party was well underway; Arlette was nose to nose with one of Winnie's friends and trying to promote her mung bean pate as a must have for the annual WI cookery book. Cedric Waterman was deep in conversation with Major Ronaldson organising their forthcoming re-enactment event that was due to take place after the Christmas festivities. Winnie was bustling around armed with plates of canapés, and blinis, trying and failing miserably to offload Arlette's vegetarian option.

"Bridget, dear, do see if anyone needs a refill, I'm afraid I'm a little tied up with the food."

"Will do Mum," she replied heading back into the fray and stealing herself for the bottom-pinchers. "'Now can I top you up Vicar?"

Anita was holding court and had attached herself to Max as the only attractive male in the room.

"I don't usually stray far from London, but I thought I'd give the provinces a try." She was telling Max and once again her mobile, permanently held in her right hand, bleeped its anxious tone. Jessica had a good instinct about people. Her mother had briefly filled her in on Anita's background, model and bit part actress in London, so she couldn't understand what this stunning young woman, with a reputedly busy life in London was doing spending Christmas in the sticks. Something didn't add up about this. Jessica went off in search of Bridget and found her in front of the Aga on the floor, breaking off lumps of French bread and feeding it to Bounder the black Labrador and his devoted companion Peggy, a Fox Terrier with attitude.

"I don't think I can stand that Anita for the whole of Christmas." Jessica moaned reaching for the kettle. "If she's not running down country life, she's huddled around her mobile. I don't think all is quite right with lady muck."

"You mean Cruella," Bridget laughed. "I overheard

her telling Arlette she thought the house was like a set from an Agatha Christie, so no prizes for guessing who will be murdered first!" Bridget got to her feet and grabbed a mug. "So, tell me all about life in Bristol." She pulled up a chair and tucked into the brie and salmon that had been left there.

After the excesses of Christmas day, the Waterman's other tradition was attending the Boxing Day Meet which despite bans on fox hunting, was still able to gather in Phoxton largely due to the fact that Tristram Hackett, owner of 500 Acre Farm, allowed the hunt full access to his land. However, having heard that hunt saboteurs were expected to be out in force this Boxing day, the Hunt aficionados' had decided to follow a dragged scent so as not to give the activists any ammunition. They could return to traditional hunting later in the year when there was likely to be far less interest.

"Wrap up warm everybody, plenty of layers." Winnie was marshalling everyone in the hall and handing out scarves and gloves.

"Stout boots are what you need Bridget, not those flimsy things." Cedric gently chastised his younger daughter whilst handing her a pair of walking boots obviously several sizes too big.

Just then Anita, resplendent in full country attire, sauntered down the staircase. From her immaculate DuBarry boots that had never seen even a hint of mud, to her jauntily placed deerstalker, she looked straight from the pages of Country Life. Even the coney rabbits' foot scarf, long-since dead, looked ready to partake in outdoor pursuits.

"I bet several animals lost their lives to produce that," Bridget remarked testily to Jessica.

"We can hardly complain," responded Jessica, "we are about to be following a blood sport after-all."

"You promised it was only a dragged scent," Bridget retorted.

After much discussion and debate about seating arrangements, largely so that Anita didn't have to bunk up in the back of the battered Land Rover, they decided to take two cars and Patrick whisked Anita off with her mobile bleeping much to the relief of the Waterman clan.

"That young woman would benefit from a bit of country living," Winnie remarked as she rammed the land rover into gear and bounced down the pot hole driveway.

Arriving at the Meet, Jessica and Bridget stood watching the horses, eager to get going, their heads flicking back, nostrils snorting, their breath curling like smoke in the frosty air. It appeared to Jessica that most of Phoxton and the surrounding villages had turned out for the Meet this Boxing Day. Bridget had been persuaded to come on the assurance that no foxes were being chased – the riders and hounds were simply following the dragged scent. The large numbers could in all probability be put down to a need for fresh air and exercise following the excesses of Christmas day, more likely than any real interest in the sport. The ground was still covered with a layer of Christmas snow, which being rarer than rocking horse poo, meant that the children were happily entertained snowballing.

Bridget's interest had been ignited when Jessica told her that James and Luke Henderson were amongst the riders. The 'Henderson boys' as they were affectionately known, were both former army servicemen who now ran Hendersons Wine Bar in town. Their reputations went before them and Bridget was keen to get a closer look.

The Sargeants arrived and Anita tiptoed around the horses, avoiding the dirty snow and trying to look interested in her surroundings but clearly out of her comfort zone.

"I used to ride, but it plays havoc with one's thigh muscles, and my face and figure are my fortune so to speak." Anita grinned at the Hunt Master.

"I had a friend, Miranda, who got 'bottom-spread' from too much time in the saddle," Bridget replied. "At least I think it was horse-riding." At which point Jessica nearly choked on her hot punch.

Two of the hounds started nudging at Anita.

"Back, back, go away!" She tried to shoo them away, but they seemed very intent on something. In true pack form, interest from one became interest from all and soon she was surrounded, screeching at the top of her voice for assistance.

"What is that scarf made of Anita?" Bridget called, noticing that they all appeared to be jumping up at her.

"Pure coney and mink," she replied proudly.

"'Well there's your problem, serves you right for wearing real fur." Bridget laughed

"Never mind that!" she screamed. "Someone do

something!" But by way of saviour the Hunt Master sounded the horn and the foxhounds swarmed to attention as the hunt were on their way.

Winnie appeared, headscarf lifting in the slight breeze, Barbour buttoned up to the neck, reminiscent of the queen at Sandringham.

"Let's all head down across the fields to the brook, if we stand on the bridge we can see them pass by and then it's only a short hop to the 'Fox and Hounds' for a winter Pimms."

"Good idea." Anita seemed relieved that although some field walking was involved it would lead to a warm pub and civilisation.

"They're orff!" Cedric Waterman called out in military fashion. "'Better hurry, we're all heading to Phoxton Bridge, get the best view from there. Good Morning Max." Cedric shook his hand then picked up his walking poles and marched off ahead.

Having negotiated the least treacherous path through the now sludge-drenched fields, and kept up with the army of country bumpkins intent on draining every last ounce of hunt fever out of themselves, Anita was relieved to see the thatched roof and white washed building ahead with the creaking sign welcoming her to the warmth of, ironically, the 'Fox and Hounds' Public House.

Unable to pick up a signal on her mobile inside, Anita was hopping from foot to foot to keep warm whilst sipping her hot Pimms outside the pub. She had to wander over to the edge of the lane to get the requisite three bars reception. Just then the hunt came thundering past in the adjacent field, taking the fence effortlessly down along the lane on the grass verge and over into the opposite fields with the hounds diving through the hedgerow after them. As Anita looked on distractedly some of the hounds appeared to stall and started circling their noses picking up a familiar scent.

"Oh! Oh!" Anita dropped her glass as one by one the hounds headed for her; she turned on her heel, cleared the fence and began running back across the field from where they had just come, closely followed by a sea of wagging tails. Unbeknownst to Anita, Hunt saboteurs, (not paparazzi as she mistakenly believed) were bringing up the rear of the group to ensure no real foxes were being chased. They too were mistaken in their belief that the hounds taking off in another direction might be a decoy and thinking a live kill might be in the offing, decided to give chase.

"'I say, Anita's frightfully fit, if she carries on the way she's going, she outrun them all – Tally Ho old girl." Winnie raised her glass, not realising that Anita was being actively pursued by the hounds and mistakenly thinking she was having a rare old time.

Jessica, catching the squeals from Anita as she came out of the pub, quickly realised that all was not well. The hunt saboteurs were clicking their cameras furiously to get the obligatory visual proof of wrongdoing and Anita who by now had reached the far corner of the field, launched herself onto the frozen pond in the hope that the hounds wouldn't venture onto the ice. In pursuit of their quarry the hounds at first tentatively approached and then haphazardly slid around as Anita on her hands and knees edged backwards her yells for help increasing as the ice began to crack.

Even the hunt saboteurs, who were merely Crispin Granger, a local placard waving leftie who jumped on any cause going in order to justify his lack of work ethic and to annoy his investment banker parents and a couple of local layabouts, realised that Anita was the sole target of the pack. He decided against trying to reach her on the ice and stood well back before any blame could be laid at their door. Crispin, never one to miss an opportunity, was immediately on his mobile to the Phoxton Gazette. 'London Model in Blood Thirsty Attack' or 'Hounds of the Phoxton Hunt' – he could work out the headline later.

"Don't just stand there, do something you paparazzi scum!" She screamed at them, still believing them to be paparazzi on the tale of a good story about a (very minor) celebrity.

"We're not paparazzi, we are official hunt saboteurs," Crispin retorted over the noise of the yapping hounds. "We should have you reported to the animal rights for wearing fur."

At that moment Anita realised the problem, she struggled to untie the coney scarf, and with her last remaining strength hurled the item across the pond at which point the hounds leapt after it and tore it to shreds.

The hunt, who had eventually realised they had lost a large proportion of their pack, could now be seen heading back towards the pub in search of their missing hounds. Jessica, Bridget and Max arrived on foot all gasping for breath having run across the field in pursuit. The ice, having given way with the weight of the hounds crashing about on it, revealed a muddy shallow pond, and Anita although sodden and humiliated, was relatively unharmed.

"I think I've twisted my ankle," she cried to Max who was nobly wading through mud to rescue her. "My beautiful scarf is in shreds," she wailed to an unsympathetic audience.

"We need to get her into the warm, and a brandy I think." Max and a reluctant Crispin supported the struggling Anita back across the field to the pub where Cedric emerged with Patrick.

"Glad to see that girl's finally getting into the spirit of things," he remarked to Patrick completely oblivious of the commotion that had just ensued.

"I could have been eaten alive!" Anita spluttered, all dignity lost now.

A very shaken Anita was given a blanket and a brandy and sat in front of a roaring fire in the pub thoroughly enjoying the limelight, now that she had forgotten the abject humiliation she had just suffered. As the brandy kicked in she revealed the reason for the persistent mobile calls and worry about the paparazzi. An affair gone wrong with a married MP in a London Borough constituency, (who despite assurances to Anita that his wife didn't understand him, she'd managed to understand him sufficiently to become pregnant) had resulted in Anita needing some time away to allow things to blow over. Said love rat MP had promised if Anita kept quiet and denied everything, should the paparazzi find her, he would make sure she got a small part in a new BBC costume drama as he had considerable influence at the Beeb. The phone calls had been to ensure she was keeping her end of the bargain and in fact, utterly dejected, she was. Jessica and Bridget always keen to fight the corner of the underdog were quick to jump to her defence now. Bridget, assistant producer for a production company in London, had some small influence that could be of use to Anita, and as for the MP, Jessica believed Anita appearing in a local newspaper, albeit for being mistakenly brought down by hounds, might be enough to dampen his ardour a little for the future.

Max, having bandaged Anita's ankle with Winnie's headscarf, was organising transportation back to the Waterman's. Just as he lifted Anita into the taxi flashbulbs went off and the local reporter stepped forward to ask Anita a few questions about her ordeal.

"I'm ready for my close-up now." She beamed. Once a diva, always a diva.

A Little Light Entertainment

The Old High Street runs through the length of the town of Flipping Bodbury, leading out to Phoxton village in one direction and Lightbury village in the other. It also provides the main traffic route to Cheltenham, passing the communal park land, cricket pitch and the Green, which is the hallowed ground providing the venue for many community activities. The Green is lovingly tended by the residents association who pride themselves on their floral displays, and the white picket fence that edges the entire area is always immaculately kept by paint-brush wielding cubs earning their DIY badges. It is a picture-postcard quintessential Cotswold town. Running parallel to the road are two rows of shops, businesses and eating establishments that are largely dependent on the yellow Cotswold stone to ensure their survival via the tourist trade.

Flipping Bodbury's first class tea shop, 'A Bit Of What You Fancy', sits on the corner of the Old High Street and the Cheltenham Road, affording its customers a wonderful view of the bustling town from its two bay fronted windows.

Elizabeth Montgomery, Lady Chair of the WI, was heaping clotted cream onto a fruit scone that was already heavily laden with butter and jam.

"No sugar for me Winnie," she informed her deputy Chair person, "I'm trying to be good." Elizabeth failed to see the irony of this as she crammed the scone into her capacious mouth.

Arlette Sargeant, the third member of the coven, yawned. For the umpteenth time she wished they were having this meeting in Hendersons Wine Bar, where she could partake of a refreshing crisp Gin and Tonic instead of lukewarm stewed Earl Grey.

"Now ladies," Elizabeth spluttered, wiping the edges of her mouth with her serviette and trying to remain ladylike as clotted cream dropped down her crimplene blouse. "I'm not sure if you are aware but I am to be incapacitated for the next few weeks, due to minor surgery." She paused, looking about her to make sure no-one was listening. The tea shop was in fact rammed to the gills with foreign visitors who were noisily consulting guide books and referring to everything as 'so quaint'. She continued in a whisper, "surgery to my down belows." She scanned the room again to make sure no-one had heard, and so missed Arlette spitting her tea back into her cup as she faked a coughing fit in order to disguise the hysterics that were welling up inside her. Again Elizabeth returned to the matter in hand,

"I am trusting you to step into the breach whilst I am away. I shall be convalescing in Stow on the Wold at my sister's." She announced this with such reverence as if she was off to outer Mongolia.

"Naturally Elizabeth, we will do everything we can to ensure the smooth running of the WI in your absence." Winnie managed to regain her composure but Arlette was still struggling.

"Really Arlette, I keep telling you to give up those cigarettes, hark at that cough they've given you." Elizabeth returned to the matter in hand. "So ladies, our annual fund-raising dinner dance will have to be organised in my absence. I am proposing that you both take on the planning of this event and report to me via my mobile telecommunication device, which will enable us to keep in contact during my recuperation."

Winnie Waterman and Arlette Sargeant liked nothing better than combining their passion for entertaining with a spot of fund-raising which really brought out the best in the residents of Flipping Bodbury and its surrounding villages. Winnie was slightly surprised at Elizabeth placing her trust in them with such a prestigious event however, with the duo in charge the stuffy, formal dinners of previous years would be a thing of the past and it would ensure a good turnout.

"Ladies nothing too outrageous please, a simple dinner, with dancing, perhaps some light entertainment, nothing too flashy. Remember a large contingent of civic dignitaries will be there." Elizabeth, whilst trying to establish some ground rules, had failed to appreciate that the civic dignitaries were often the worst behaved once they had a couple of drinks inside them. Further instructions followed, with Elizabeth informing them that The Malmsbury Spa Hotel had already been booked for the event and a meeting arranged with Olivia Beckwith, event's organiser for Crossley Hotels, the following day. She continued, "The rest is up to you ladies, but please remember that you carry the responsibility of upholding the good name of The Flipping Bodbury WI in your hands." Winnie and Arlette looked at each other and smiled sweetly, offering reassurances galore.

Once Elizabeth was safely packed off to have her nether regions attended to at a private hospital in Cheltenham, Winnie and Arlette scheduled all further WI planning meetings at Hendersons Wine Bar where they felt their creative juices flowed more freely once lubricated with a little alcohol.

"What are we raising money for exactly?" asked Maud Beechy, a stickler for regulations, just like Elizabeth and a possible mole in the planning camp. Winnie knew that when it came to the nitty gritty of planning the cabaret Maud would need to be excluded from the meetings or they'd never keep things secret from Elizabeth.

"We are trying to raise enough money to provide heating for the Church hall. Those poor little brownies go home with blue fingers and toes after a Thursday evening in the winter." Winnie explained to the assembled committee which included herself, Arlette her co-organiser, Maud Beechy main protagonist, Candice Wells and her partner Maureen Parker and finally Drew and Blair Bantham, affiliate members on the basis that firstly they were male, but secondly they were gay and invaluable members of the group. "However," continued Winnie, "if there is enough money left over we are hoping to pay for the Reverend

Hopeswell to have a new prosthetic leg." At this Drew and Blair spat Campari across the assembled group.

"What!" Drew choked.

"Oh, yes Drew, haven't you heard him clicking up and down the aisle as he leads in the procession? It's bad enough when it's the wedding march but in the silence of a funeral procession it is really quite irreverent when he sounds like a Nazi marching along." Winnie imparted this information completely straight-faced.

"His current artificial leg is a wooden one he's had for decades; it's probably out of the ark." Arlette added.

"If it is it'll be worth hanging onto!" Blair spluttered and even Maud saw the funny side at last.

"So there we are then," continued Winnie undaunted, "a dinner, dancing and a cabaret. Is everyone in agreement?" She looked around at her fellow organisers.

"What type of cabaret will it be?" Maud asked, looking decidedly dubious.

"Something tasteful," Winnie responded, "you can rely on me." This was exactly what worried Maud, so whilst everyone else stayed for another drink, she hurried off to report back to Elizabeth.

The following week a more covert sub-sub-committee meeting was held in a room at the back of 'The Cock and Bull Story', owned by Drew and Blair. The subterfuge was to ensure that Maud Beechy knew nothing of the arrangements for the only agenda item up for discussion, the cabaret. As Winnie and Arlette had already met with Olivia Beckwith at the

Malmsbury Spa to organise the food and drink required, this left the most pressing matter of the entertainment to be decided.

"Can we expect posh nosh at the Malms?" Drew enquired, always interested in his food.

"Certainly not, we will be having a hearty meal using locally produced ingredients; Beef Wellington; made from cattle slaughtered at Tristram Hacketts farm." Winnie never one to mince her words, stated matter-of-factly.

"Oh, Winnie, you've quite put me off that now," moaned Drew.

"Well in that case you'll have to go for the veggie option, Mung Bean Casserole, from Arlette's very own recipe, that the chef at Malms has agreed to follow." Winnie noticed that this suggestion was met with equally unfavourable looks. "Anyway, moving on to the matter in hand; the cabaret. Do we have any suggestions?" She addressed the group.

"How about a magic act?" Drew asked. "We could nominate some of the more tedious old duffers to be vanished."

"No, Drew, you're really not helping," Winnie gently chastised.

"How about an auction, people could bid to spend an evening with David Beckham," Blair proudly suggested.

"Does anybody know David Beckham in order to get him to agree to this?" Arlette interjected as the voice of reason.

"Well perhaps not actually David Beckham, but between us we must know at least one Z list celebrity?" he responded hopefully, looking wounded that his idea was failing.

"Actually, I already have an idea," Winnie interrupted the silence. "What about a tribute band?"

"I went to see an Abba tribute band once," Candice hesitatingly offered, "they weren't very good, for one thing they were all Swedish and I just couldn't quite get into it." This last left everyone very confused.

"Abba were Swedish Candice," Drew pointed out.

"Oh," She replied, "Perhaps they were better than I realised then."

"As I was saying." Winnie was desperately trying to keep on track. "I do know of a tribute band that just might be interested. They are Bootleg Village People."

"Just because they are alcoholics is no reason to think we shouldn't support them." Arlette was now thoroughly unconvinced by this idea.

"No Arlette dear, bootleg as in a copy of something, not contraband booze. The Village People were gay icons of the early 80s. Everyone knows YMCA, and as there is an 80s revival going on at the moment, I think it might be very popular." Blair was becoming more interested by the moment.

Winnie's daughter Bridget, when she was at university doing Theatre Studies, had been friends with a group of lads who had formed a tribute band in order to help fund their university fees. Bridget, who had since dropped out of uni, offered to contact them and book the gig. There followed further discussions and as no alternative suggestions were likely to be approved by Elizabeth, a decision was made to hire the band. Winnie stressed to the group the necessity to keep the information offered to Maud about the cabaret act to a bare minimum, and just to be sure, she neglected to inform them that the act was a touch risqué, so that nobody would crack under pressure. Over the next week tickets were designed and printed, and went on sale in all the local establishments. With Olivia safely in charge of arrangements at the Malmsbury there was little else that the committee needed to do other than publicise the event to ensure that the tickets sold.

Everything was running along smoothly with a tremendous sale of tickets, until Winnie received a call from Rob Gullitt, the lead singer with the tribute band, who called themselves 'YnotMCA'. He called to say that three members of the band had been arrested at a so-called peaceful demonstration in London, protesting about university top-up fees, and would still be detained at Her Majesty's pleasure on the evening of the dinner dance. Winnie was straight on the phone to Arlette, who called an emergency meeting at Hendersons to work out a fallback option.

The following morning Winnie woke with a sore throat and a thumping headache. As she tried to move, every bone in her body was throbbing, and it was the most she could do to pick up the phone and dial Arlette.

"No Winnie dear, stay put, take paracetamol and get Cedric to look after *you* for once. There is nothing to worry about, I'll take care of everything." Arlette hung up having reassured her friend. She thought, not for the first time, that Winnie who had the flu jab each year, always came down with some form of lurgy and yet she, Arlette, who relied on 40 cigarettes a day, remained fit and healthy. Always a star in a crisis she set off to see Drew and Blair.

"Well as I see it there's only one thing to do," stated Blair later that day in Hendersons.

"You mean cancel the cabaret?" Drew looked shocked.

"No, of course not. We'll make up the numbers ourselves." Once more Arlette nearly choked on her drink.

"Well you can count me out." Drew looked horrified at the very idea.

"Drew my lovely, you have many admirable qualities, but even you as a genuinely gay man would be useless in a YMCA tribute band. You can't sing and you definitely can't dance." Drew, who should have been offended, was actually completely relieved to be relinquished from that particular threat.

"So who do you suggest then?" Arlette enquired, bewildered.

"Leave it to me Arlette. Rest assured Blair Bantham knows best in this instance. A week on Saturday there will be a full line up on that stage, I guarantee. Now if you'll excuse me I have people to see." Blair's hidden diva was suddenly in full swing as he grabbed his Filofax, and planted a quick kiss on Drew's balding head as he swept out of the bar.

"That is my Blair at his best," Drew preened as he headed to the bar for refills.

As Winnie recovered from influenza, brought on in part from living in a house full of damp and draughts, she began to eagerly anticipate the dinner dance, but with Blair remaining tight-lipped about the cabaret she was a little anxious too. Blair on the other hand was in his element. He had enlisted the help of two of his closest friends in the town, and for the past ten days they had held secret practice sessions in the church hall late at night. Rod Gullit, the YnotMCA lead singer, had explained to Blair where to find a video of one of their performances so that they could learn the moves. Having met Winnie and Arlette, he found them good sports; he was anxious to make the evening as special as he could for the WI. The replacement band members were all considerably different shapes and sizes to the original members, so Blair had drafted in Molly and Dolly Masters who ran 'So Sew' in the town to do some alterations to the costumes. The spinster pair were delighted to be part of the secret, and to ensure the modesty of the new recruits they had made them face masks to hide their identities. (This being the only way that Blair had managed to persuade them to perform.)

Arriving at the Malmsbury hotel on the evening of the dance, Winnie was thrilled to see that, true to her word, Olivia had pulled out all the stops and the Cavanaugh room looked beautiful. Formal tables gave way to the wooden dance floor complete with several hanging disco balls, and at the far end of the room the temporary stage was draped with red velvet curtains edged in brocade.

"Perfect," Winnie sighed as she looked around.

"We are all set to go Winnie." Olivia Beckwith was placing the seating plan at the entrance to the room. "The lighting engineers were here earlier for a sound check so everything is ready." Olivia had sneakily peeped in at the rehearsal earlier and could now hardly wait for the evening to begin.

"I'll just powder my nose before people start to arrive." Winnie headed off to the ladies room checking that Cedric was still positioned at the hotel bar and hadn't sloped off home as was his want on these occasions.

The room began to fill up with familiar faces. Tray after tray of bucks fizz came out, and the noise level of chatter began to increase signalling that everyone was relaxing and enjoying themselves. To Winnie and Arlette's utter amazement Elizabeth Montgomery entered the room on the arm of Major Ronaldson who looked dapper in his evening dress. They headed straight over.

"Good evening ladies," Elizabeth immediately took in their shocked expressions. "You didn't think I would miss the highlight of the social calendar did you?" she mocked.

"How lovely to see you Elizabeth, are you feeling up to this?" Winnie managed to ask whilst reaching out for yet another bucks fizz from a passing tray.

"I have enjoyed a splendid recuperation with my sister, and the Major has promised to stay by my side in case I tire." Elizabeth was clearly enjoying his undivided attention.

The dinner gong sounded, and Winnie grateful for the opportunity to escape, grabbed Arlette to find their husbands and their table. The meal which was a great success was followed by a brief address from Elizabeth, and an even briefer thank you from Reverend Hopeswell for the turnout, which would surely mean the central heating could be fitted to his church hall. Winnie couldn't help but notice that he rattled through his speech, very unlike the way he dawdled through his sermons, and made a hasty exist as soon as it was done. Dancing followed and as Cedric remained firmly planted at the bar, Winnie annoyed all the younger women in the room by grabbing her friend Jamie Henderson and dragging him onto the floor. Arlette too was searching for Patrick, who normally loved a boogie but had completely disappeared also.

Elizabeth and the Major took to the floor for the rumba. Reminding herself that for once she wasn't leading, and it being a long time since a man had taken her in his arms, Elizabeth tentatively began to move. They soon settled into a rhythm with the Major looking debonair in his tux. Forgetting the people around them, they began to increase the pace, and as the Major twirled Elizabeth out with his left arm and threw his head back in a flamboyant gesture befitting the music; his top set of false teeth flew out of his mouth. Thanks to an uncharacteristic display of dexterity he was able to catch his airborne molars unnoticed by Elizabeth, who was still completing her twirl. He quickly pushed them back in; vowing to find a more reliable polygrip the next day. Jamie and Luke Henderson, watching from the bar whilst both trying to pull Nicky Butler, a bar maid with the most ample assets, nearly choked on their beer. Elizabeth, oblivious to the incident, was still floating around the dance floor.

The four piece band, The Jolly Fiddlers, that had been playing all evening finished their session with a resounding samba, and were given enthusiastic applause for all their efforts. As they moved swiftly to the bar the guests returned to their seats as Elizabeth took to the microphone once more.

"Ladies, Gentlemen and distinguished guests." She particularly looked at the WI review committee as she addressed her audience, "I'm sure you'll all agree that we have had a super dinner and we've seen some excellent movers on the dance floor. I'd like you to sit back now and prepare to be entertained by our cabaret act." Applause followed this and Elizabeth withdrew from the stage as the lights dimmed and the curtains drew back, the familiar (to some) refrain of the icon YMCA tune began, as the copycat Village People took to the stage to the sound of catcalls and wolf whistles.

The familiar dance routine brought the audience to their feet as the professional band members strutted their stuff alongside the new recruits, (very apt considering the song lyrics) who were only slightly less foot-sure but certainly not lacking in camp swagger. Everyone was enjoying themselves thoroughly, and Winnie and Arlette were straining to recognise the three mystery members. Arlette, who had decided that Patrick must be keeping Cedric company in the adjoining lounge area, was disappointed he was missing this hilarious act which undoubtedly he would have loved. As the number came to its end, the audience shouted for an encore and much to Winnie and Arlette's amazement they got exactly that. The familiar sound of a Hot Chocolate song began to play,

"How funny Winnie, my Patrick has been humming this all week," Arlette informed her.

The costumed band members on stage got into their places as Rod Gullit belted out the famous tune. Winnie was trying to remember what the movie was called that had re-ignited the songs popularity, as everyone began to sway and sing along. As the number neared the end and the sound of ripping Velcro could be heard, Rod sang out "I believe in miracles," their costumes came away in their hands with only the masks still in place to prevent recognition. At the front of the line-up stood the Reverend Hopeswell, a dead giveaway as he was the only one wearing Damart to shield his modesty, but was clearly recognisable with a red bow tied around his wooden leg!! The shrieks of delight could be heard for miles... Winnie and Arlette glanced round to see Elizabeth fall into a dead faint into the Major's thankfully still strong arms.

Blair raced off the stage into the arms of his most adoring fan.

"You did brilliantly," Drew told him gushingly.

"I did didn't I?" Blair gushed, "and what's more dear Drew I get to keep the costume!" He gathered up the American policeman's uniform and firmly placed the helmet on Drew's head. "Such fun!" He shrieked as they headed home.

The official WI Monitoring Committee headed back onto their minibus some time later amid much chatter and high spirits. Winnie was struggling to pour Cedric into the Landrover, alongside Arlette, who had found Patrick backstage (albeit in a somewhat dishevelled state). They were both delighted to overhear one of the committee declare it was the best WI Annual Dinner Dance to date! Winnie hoped that Elizabeth would appreciate this compliment – but somehow she very much doubted it...

A Mouse Fortuitous Calamity

The first planning meeting for the Flipping Bodbury Women's Institute annual theatrical extravaganza took place on a cold October afternoon in the home of Winnie Waterman. A long standing member of the WI, she was a passionate fund raiser and although a little scatty, she was a generous hostess. The committee members were assembled in the drawing room of Winnie's delightful Cotswold home which nestled in several acres of unspoilt countryside. A little ragged around the edges, not unlike its owners, this baronial home of great proportions was filled with clutter and the occasional antique and exuded charm and a welcoming atmosphere. The dogs lazed toasting before a roaring fire whose heat belied the lack of proper central heating. Winnie wandered around supplying sherry and homemade nibbles whilst Elizabeth Montgomery, Lady Chair, formerly called the meeting to order.

"Now then ladies," she began, tapping her spoon against her glass for attention. "Following the trials and tribulations of The Pirates of Penzance last year, I felt that despite it finally ending in a great triumph, we might tackle something a little less demanding for this year's production." This was generally met with nods of agreement by the ensemble. "Yes, a little am dram I think is in order, and so I have selected 'The Mousetrap'." Elizabeth put down her glass and looked around for a reaction.

"I think that's a splendid idea but do you think we are up to it?" Maud Beechy famed for her negativity was always the first to question their abilities in all things thespian.

"Well as usual I have enlisted the help of Theodore Bartlett, he is happy to produce us again but we will need to find a replacement director this year as Larry is still not fully recovered from his little breakdown following lasts years production." Elizabeth was keen to gloss over this particular uncomfortable situation.

"Well as a matter of fact I have given this some thought," announced Winnie, in an unusually forthright manner. "As you know my Bridget is home at the moment." This comment was met with general murmurs and commiserations. "And I rather felt that having almost completed a Theatre Studies degree she might be the ideal replacement for Larry." Winnie's daughter, Bridget, had been having an affair with one of her lecturers who had promised her that he would leave his wife, however, unfortunately for Bridget the wife announced she was having their first child at the late age of 47, and all of his promises forgotten he dumped Bridget like a hot potato leaving her heartbroken. Bridget had been welcomed home like the prodigal daughter as the Waterman's had rallied around their little girl.

"Shall we vote on that proposal then," chipped in Arlette Sargeant, Winnie's best friend of forty years standing. "All those in favour of Bridget being director, raise your hands now." She didn't wait for everyone to comply, anxious to ensure that Bridget was given the task as she believed a project was just what she needed to get over her broken heart. "Brilliant, well that's a resounding agreement."

General discussions then took place as to who had seen the famous production that had been running for 85 years at the St Martin's Theatre, and who might be cast in what role until Elizabeth once again called for quiet.

"One further disappointment, I'm afraid, is that of course our dear friend and colleague Beattie will not be able to take the female lead this year. Her double hip replacement went well but she will not be treading the boards anytime soon." General murmurs of regret followed this announcement.

"I still think she only got the role of the Pirate King last year because she had a natural moustache and moles, my baritone was much richer," whispered Maureen Parker to Arlette as she reached for another vol-au-vent. Maureen was the token lesbian of the group, she had been with her "partner" Candice for many years and only the most naïve members of the group could fail to realise they were romantically attached. Maureen, the butch of the two, was always the first to volunteer to set up tables at the fete or move scenery and her ability to drive a fork lift truck had come in handy many times over the years.

It was a successful planning meeting with much

banter and hilarity and Winnie moved on to serving tea and cakes. Such was the reluctance of everyone to leave the warmth of both the fire and the company of friends. Elizabeth, amongst the hullabaloo had managed to confirm that open auditions would take place at the end of the month in the town hall, and the local brownie pack would make and distribute posters inviting anyone interested to come along. Eventually the group dispersed out into the cold evening and Winnie ushered her reluctant dogs out into the bracing air for their evening walk, delighted with the prospect of a project for Bridget.

After three evenings of auditions the production team were beginning to lose heart, and on the final evening they were casting the role of Mrs Boyle, described as 'a generally unpleasant woman who is dissatisfied with everyone and everything'.

"Should be fairly easy to pick from any of the older WI members," Winnie sniggered to Bridget.

At 7.00pm the church hall doors were opened and a steady stream of hopefuls entered. They were seated at the back of the hall to be called to act out a scene before the top table panel. The panel was led by Elizabeth Montgomery who took her role very seriously as Lady Chair; next to her was Theodore Bartlett, Producer, whose main claim to fame was running the panto season at the RSC one year, but he made it seem as though he was Lord Olivier himself, such was his theatrical manner. Next to Theodore sat Bridget Waterman, as Director, having been enlisted to help by her mother she reluctantly agreed, partly through boredom of being back at home and partly to placate her mother whose disappointment in her recent troubles had been bravely masked. Bridget was feeling less than confident about the cast members chosen so far and was desperately hoping for an officious, large lady to cast in the role of Mrs Boyle in order to add some depth to the ensemble. Finally, resplendent in velvet lounge suits and cravats at the far end of the table were Blair and Drew Bantham, local secondhand bookshop owners, "The Cock and Bull Story" was a thriving small business. Their artistic temperaments were worthy of any Broadway Theatre Company, nevermind a local am dram set-up, but their forte was scenery and for this they were beyond compare. Drew and Blair's creation of a flying pink ship landing on the stage for the Pirates of Penzance was now a legendary and talk of this phenomenon rivalled the impact of the flying car in Chitty Chitty Bang Bang in the West End.

By the time the casting panel had seen five terrible candidates Bridget was truly losing heart, when a booming voice from the back of the hall interrupted her gloom,

"I've been waiting to be called for half an hour. I have dinner reservations in 15 minutes at The Brasserie, I insist on being heard now or I shall take my leave." Joan Sidewell stood up, clearly a force to be reckoned with.

"Thank goodness for that." Bridget nudged Theodore in the side, "Our Mrs Boyle has just entered the room!"

Two weeks later the WI ladies had been summoned to a mass painting session at the Church Hall, painting the back drop for the stage which showed a large, country house sitting room with French doors leading to the terrace where snow could be seen falling. Maureen Parker, tall thickset and dressed as usual in cheesecloth blouse and denim dungarees, was merrily hammering away at the support posts for the back drop with a mouthful of tacks and thoroughly at home with the task. She was closely watched by her adoring partner Candice, a total contrast; small, bubbly and blonde who hated getting her hands dirty but was in her element arranging pieces of furniture to give the 1930s feel that the play required. Bridget and Elizabeth Montgomery were busy designing the posters to advertise the forthcoming production. Elizabeth was stressing over the cast order, not wanting to offend anyone but at the same time anxious to stick to protocol. Candice, glancing over Bridget's shoulder remarked cheekily,

"Ronnie Webster won't be pleased to be under Joan, he'll want equal billing at least."

"Just because he's paid for the stage to be installed he can't ride roughshod over us. Some of us have been doing this for years, he's walked in and got a lead role." Drew was always quick to start a quarrel.

"Well speak for yourself Drewie but I've always liked the older man myself," replied Blair being deliberately provocative. Such was the nature of the pair that they had to stir up trouble.

"Shall we have tits on the bird table, after all it is winter and they'd be searching for food?" said Drew. Winnie and Arlette sniggered. "Straight men don't have the monopoly ladies, I've seen a few pairs in my time, and I'm not talking Conference pears." He returned to his stitching.

"How are you getting on Blair?" Drew asked looking up from his painting.

"I've just had the odd small prick, but apart from that I'm doing fine," he replied his face the picture of innocence.

"Oh! You should be so lucky," Drew replied throwing a paintbrush at Blair.

"Now you're just getting filthy Drew Bantham, let's break for lunch and restore a little decorum." Blair exited stage right and returned buckling under the weight of a wicker hamper complete with gingham cloth. "Grub's up ladies." He proceeded to hand round plates of bloater paste sandwiches and egg and cress bridge rolls to the delight of all the helpers.

By the time the dress rehearsals were underway Bridget's enthusiasm for the task was beginning to wane. Despite being grateful for the distraction from her dire personal life she now felt exhausted by the enormity of the task. The 'Bodbury Players' as she affectionately called them were only a small cast and crew but what they lacked in numbers they more than made . up for in demands, and juggling the diverse temperaments was taking its toll on her. Throughout the day there had been numerous costume traumas and much to-ing and fro-ing between Bridget and the wardrobe mistresses, Molly and Dolly Masters, spinster sisters who run "So Sew", the sewing shop in town. By late afternoon Bridget was flagging and called the whole cast onto the stage in whatever attire they had managed to put together in order to give them the once over and their final instructions for the run through.

However, backstage the cast were greeted by a lot of giggling, courtesy of Drew and Blair who had been celebrating the successful completion of the superb scenery with a bottle of Sloe Gin, a present from one of the WI ladies who misunderstood the alcoholic content of the beverage.

Trying and failing to look disapproving; Winnie Waterman was about to suggest some very black coffee, when an almighty crash was heard coming from the rear of the stage followed by a high pitched scream.

"What in God's name is going on!" cried Bridget, climbing onto the stage and hurrying into the wings where she was closely followed by Drew and Blair still sniggering from their excesses. The group were greeted by the sight of Joan Sidewell playing the part of the formidable Mrs Boyle who appeared to have gone straight through one of the floorboards and was flailing about like a newly emerged seedling in the wind.

"Somebody get me out!" she shouted, her face puce with embarrassment. "I think I've broken something; call an ambulance at once!" Drew and Blair fell about laughing inappropriately, unable to contain themselves any longer.

"When we said break a leg old girl, we didn't mean it literally," Drew spluttered. Bridget turned and fixed them with a hard stare.

"Oh grow up you two can't you see she's hurt and she's due to perform next week." With that she slammed down her clipboard and dialled 999.

As the dreadful news was filtered back to the

assembled cast everyone began to view this as the beginning of the end. With only a week to go and no main character Bridget could see all her hard work going to waste. Joan had left the stage on a stretcher bound for Cheltenham General.

Handing round mugs of steaming tea to cope with the shock, Winnie and Arlette busied themselves with cheering everyone up.

"Bridget, I wonder if I might have a word?" called Arlette as Bridget was desperately thinking of possible replacements from the remaining WI motley crew.

"Arlette is it important? Theodore and I need to try to think of someone to stand in." Bridget was noticeably short with Arlette.

"Well actually I just might be able to help with that young lady," responded Arlette. "I have a friend who owes me a favour. I dog sat recently for her pug, Walter, whilst she was away filming James Bond (a delightful little dog but suffers with terrible gas). I happen to know that she is temporarily out of work, or resting as the thespians say, because they can't get the money for the new film; another victim of the recession." Bridget looked more and more irritated as Arlette rambled on. "Anyway, shall I give her a call and see if she would do us the honour." Arlette waited for a response

"Oh, you may as well give it a go," replied Bridget non-committedly, "What part did she play in James Bond, was it just a walk on role or did she have lines?"

"She had quite a big part actually. I think her character is known by an initial instead of a name."

Arlette looked a little confused.

Suddenly Bridget swung round and gave Arlette her full attention.

"Are we talking about a national treasure here?" she asked spilling her tea.

"Yes dear. I think you might be right. Trudy and I were at school together but she went on to Rada, we've always kept in touch, although she is rather busy these days." Arlette continued picking up the empty mugs unaware of the faces staring at her.

Jaws dropped all around the assembled group on stage who by now had twigged that Arlette's friend was none other than Dame Trudy Trench herself, the queen of thespian land. Bridget was quizzing Arlette as to whether she thought Dame Trudy would really consider helping them out, but Arlette seemed convinced that she would be as good as her word and disappeared off to make the call. Drew and Blair were practically apoplectic with excitement, Dame Trudy being a gay icon.

"Dame Trudy was an excellent Queen Victoria in that film, with the comedian, I'm sure she can handle our Mrs Boyle," announced Elizabeth Montgomery to Bridget, who thought these WI ladies were really getting above themselves now by checking the credentials of such a star!

Arlette was indeed 'as good as her word', and Dame Trudy having checked her schedule was able to commit to doing the performance.

Flipping Bodbury was well and truly gripped in Dame Trudy fever by the eve of the performance. The great Dame herself was staying with Arlette, and learning her lines whilst constantly being interrupted by members of the WI.

"I've never been so popular!" Arlette remarked to Winnie, "Not only do the cast and production team keep popping in but all the busybody blue rinse brigade as well." Secretly she was thrilled to have her famous friend under her roof and was martialling all the visitors with great efficiency. Dame Trudy had been only too glad to give up a weekend to support her old friend Arlette, and she was even more delighted with the part of Mrs Boyle, the Mousetrap was a play she had yet to appear in.

Jessica Simmonds, one of the more streetwise of the local Guide pack, had been responsible for putting up the poster advertising campaign for the production, and had secretly sold the story of the famous understudy to the Daily Mail which resulted in the paparazzi descending on the town. Tickets had sold out and all the local businesses were doing a roaring trade with the additional footfall through the village. Even Joan, leg in plaster up to her thigh, was determined to watch the performance from her wheelchair and admire her famous understudy. Jessica had headed off into Cheltenham to buy a pair of Jimmy Choos on the proceeds to wear at the wrap party!

Drew and Blair Bantham had contacted all their buddies to come and ogle at Dame Trudy, and were in a constant quiver of excitement, bustling around finalising the scenery and winding everyone up. The rest of the cast were however feeling the pressure and Nancy Clayton (playing the part of Mrs Ralston the young wife running the guest house where all the action takes place) was struggling with her lines, largely due to the formidable presence of the Dame.

"I just know I'm going to dry up," she kept wailing.

Drew jumped in immediately to offer the benefit of his wisdom.

"Whenever I'm in a tricky situ I just say to myself in the words of the great Larry Grayson, 'take a deep breath and sock it to them with knobs on'".

"Did he actually say that?" asked Nancy still despairing.

"Well words to that effect, I think it was Larry or perhaps it was Danny La Ru, but anyway the point is just get stuck in and you'll be fine." Drew felt that having imparted his wise words his work was done, and so wandered off to check that all his props were in order.

Phillip Greenaway, local lothario and estate agent was playing the part of Nancy's husband, but his constant leering made it even more difficult for her to concentrate on delivering her lines. The fact that they were supposed to be in the first flush of love enabled him to take full advantage of leching. As Bridget watched them have their final run-through from the wings she was feeling guilty for inflicting Phillip on her friend.

The enormity of the task ahead was taking its toll on most of the cast and the awareness that the nation's press were there too made matters worse, albeit that they were only interested in Dame Trudy. Winnie and

Arlette circulated back stage in order to offer last minute advice and calming words along with a slug from their hip flasks. However, as soon as Bridget caught sight of the pair she confiscated the flasks and banished them both to the costume room out of harm's way.

When the curtain finally went up Theodore Bartlett, who had done little for the past few days but suck up to Dame Trudy and name drop shamelessly, sat in the front row with the sole aim of gazing at one of his idols instead of being backstage supporting his cast. The first half was slow to start but with the arrival of the character of Mrs Boyle the audience picked up and it seemed the rest of the cast could feel the upsurge of interest and raised their game. By and large the cast muddled through with some elements of success, and Arlette noted that Dame Trudy played her part brilliantly but ensured that she didn't steal the limelight, and encouraged and brought out the best in her fellow thespians rather than outshining them too brightly. When the curtain finally came down after two curtain calls and the presentation of a beautiful bouquet to Dame Trudy, the cast called Bridget onto the stage to acknowledge the skills of the director, and Theodore suddenly regretted not having been backstage to share in the glory. Elizabeth Montgomery Lady Chair of the WI had been appointed as spokesperson.

"Ladies and Gentlemen, and members of the press." She gazed out at the sea of faces and took great delight at the honour of making her speech. "I would like you to join with me in thanking the great Dame Trudy for stepping in at such short notice and saving the day. In this instance breaking her leg was probably the luckiest thing that Joan could have done for Flipping Bodbury WI." A round of applause followed general titters from the audience and the fury on Joan's face quickly told Elizabeth this had not been taken as the compliment it had meant to be and she knew she was in for trouble at the next WI meeting.

As the cast left the stage Arlette informed everyone that Hendersons Wine Bar were laying on an after show party to which all were invited. Reporters were assembled at the entrance to the town hall and it had taken Elizabeth Montgomery's full booming voice to inform them that Dame Trudy was resting following her exhausting performance and would not be speaking to the press.

Winnie found Bridget backstage collecting together her script and programme which Dame Trudy had kindly autographed.

"Darling it was a marvellous performance, the WI have raised hundreds, well done everyone enjoyed it." She hugged her daughter tightly.

"Oh mum, I'm actually going to miss this lot now, I've got quite used to their cranky ways and all the tittle-tattle and falling out, whatever will I do with myself?" She shuffled her papers looking downcast.

"Well, it's funny you should mention that, Trudy tells me she has a director friend who is looking for a trainee assistant; he's going to give you a call." Winnie watched Bridget's jaw drop. "And I was going to ask if you fancied directing our next Am Dram at Easter, we were thinking of doing The Importance of Being Ernest, did I mention that I went to school with Dame

Maggie Smith, she owes me a favour." Winnie's eyes twinkled.

"Oh Mum!" Bridget laughed, putting her arm around Winnie's shoulder. "I think I need a drink!"

CAST LIST FOR THE MOUSE TRAP

Bridget Waterman	Director
Theodore Bartlett	Producer
Elizabeth Montgomery	Marketing (with help of Brownies & Guides)
Joan Sidewell	Mrs Boyle Guest (then played by the great Dame Trudy)
Phillip Greenaway	Mr Ralston (Guest House owner)
Nancy Clayton	Mrs Ralston (His wife)
Ronnie Webster	Mr Paravincini (Guest)
Candice Wells	Miss Casewell (Guest)
Patrick Sargeant	Christopher Wren (Guest)
Major Ronaldson	Sergeant Trotter (Policeman)

A Town of Two Halves

The residents of the Cotswold town of Flipping Bodbury were nothing if not enthusiastic about attending social events together. They would turn out en-mass for the opening of an envelope if they thought that free booze, nibbles and a dispute might be likely to ensue. So when a notice went up announcing a planning meeting to look into the possibility of town twinning with a town in Europe it was natural to expect a lively turnout. All the usual suspects arrived in their droves so that Major Ronaldson, tweed wearing figurehead of the project, feared that health and safety regulations were being flouted as people crammed into every available inch of the conference room in the town hall. Seated at the top table were the crème de la crème of local dignitaries, or in some instances do-gooding busybodies. Major Ronaldson had served in the Light Infantry and had a distinguished career before retiring to his birthplace and becoming a prominent figure in the town. Warwick Portillo was seated to his right, formerly a local Conservative councillor and currently an acting magistrate, firmly believes in bringing fresh interest to the town. Warwick had previously lost his seat at the last election due to his far right extremist views; not only did he want to bring back corporal punishment he was in favour of floggings in the street! His wife, the considerably younger, Francine mingled with the WI ladies and frequently glanced at her husband to reassure him that she was both enjoying herself and supporting his campaign and was aware of his ever watchful presence. Warwick was considering putting his name forward as a candidate at the next local parliamentary election and was anxious to capitalise on the popularity of his attractive wife, but was sensible enough to keep a close eye on who else was appreciating her.

"Glad you're here Truman. What do you know about pre-nups?" Warwick moved his chair closer to his friend.

"Is there trouble in paradise?" Truman had always been a tad jealous of Warwick's enviable marital situation.

"No, no. A friend of mine was recently taken to the cleaners by his wife of two years (and twenty his junior) and it made me a little nervous that's all." He rather too hastily responded.

"Come and see me next week, we'll have lunch." This was Truman's knowing reply. He would advise his friend and take some comfort from the fact that the grass wasn't always greener on the other side. Marjorie, Truman's wife, had her faults but she was loyal and they rubbed along pretty well together. His days of fecklessness were long past him. Truman, a retired solicitor who had just been appointed town Mayor, was accompanied on his right by Elizabeth Montgomery,

Lady Chair of the WI, a staunch supporter of the towns good name, indeed a grand supporter of the Cotswolds and middle England in general. Elizabeth was officious and bossy but her WI ladies forgave her for these attributes as she was also well meaning and genuinely concerned about the Townsfolk. Consistently dressed in her box pleat tweed skirts, cream silk blouses and long sensible cardigans, she appeared of good stock but was in serious need of a Gok Wan makeover. Elizabeth placed herself between the Major and the Mayor and immediately began talking in earnest about her latest WI plans.

The town hall was beginning to fill up with unlikely town twinning supporters, who were simply there for the free wine and cheese to be supplied by wine bar owners Jamie and Luke Henderson. They were keen on the town twinning idea simply because of the additional footfall through the only wine bar in town. At the back of the hall a token gesture of resistance to the whole plan was led by Crispin Granger, a sandal wearing, deodorant-free, placard waving eco warrior who believed that tourism, particularly air travel, to be the biggest single contributor to the destruction of the ozone layer. He had gathered together a small band of like-minded followers who had either dropped out of university and were relying on Mummy and Daddy's handouts, or those who had simply never done a day's work in their lives and need a good cause to justify their laziness and existence, and which generally seemed to require that they never had a wash.

Major Ronaldson banged his gavel on the top table several times in order to start the meeting.

"Order, order," he began in the manner more fitting of a parliamentary debate. "Ladies and Gentleman, we the Committee, appreciate the enormous turn out this evening which as ever shows a tremendous level of commitment that residents have towards the prosperity of Flipping Bodbury." He paused momentarily to consult his notes, typed in double line spacing and huge font to allow for clarity, such was his reluctance to submit to spectacles despite his poor eyesight. "I will begin by introducing my fellow panel members as the Brownies, kindly on loan donated by Brown Owl, distribute information packs pertaining to the submission process for Town Twinning and all relevant documents for tonight's meeting." Penelope Wainthrop, Brown Owl, never missed an opportunity for her girls to earn a badge, and she shooed them along the rows of townsfolk. The committee required ten representatives of the town and affiliated villages to visit the proposed town abroad should the submission be accepted. Therefore, when Major Ronaldson called for volunteers a stampede ensued and the top table were in danger of being shunted into the rear wall.

During the hullabaloo that accompanied these nominations Crispin took his opportunity and climbed onto one of the now free chairs and began to chant his disapproval against increasing the town's carbon footprint.

"Save the planet, save our Earth!

Just say No!

No more tourism is the way to go".

A general murmur of disapproval met the half-hearted demonstration and it was the older generation who rose to respond.

"Do pipe down Crispin, you old windbag," Winnie tutted.

"Change the record," chorused Arlette. "Too much time on his hands," she muttered to Winnie.

What the demonstration had lacked in poetry it more than made up for in simplicity, but unfortunately just as one or two members of the audience were beginning to notice this insignificant protest, the Henderson brothers arrived with the caterers. The diversion of free wine and cheese meant that the demonstrators lost any chance of gaining support from the crowd. Crispin, sensing defeat, put down his placard and was soon seen hanging about the buffet table quite happy to devour the free food along with the other less ethical members of the public. Little more was achieved at the meeting than a show of support for the project but it was a town gathering as good as any other.

The following month Major Ronaldson received a letter awarding twinning with a town in Europe. The destination was to remain unknown to the selected delegates in order to ensure no bribery took place. The Major as head of the group was under instruction to keep the exact location secret, however, Elizabeth Montgomery couldn't help but notice that he seemed slightly anxious, and less than his usual non-fazeable self.

"Anything I can help you with Major?" Elizabeth

had asked when she had quite literally bumped into the Major coming out of the post office, his mind had clearly been on other things.

"My dear Elizabeth," he began, heaving a great sigh, "I feel I may have bitten off more than I can chew this time. I only hope that the town we are being twinned with is worthy of affiliation with our beautiful Cotswold gem."

So a somewhat reserved Major Ronaldson sat drinking his tea and finishing a second piece of toast, whilst reviewing the selection of delegates on the day of the impending trip. Not for the first time did he consider the council may have made a mistake opening it up to the general public. On a positive note there were a couple of names he could rely on completely when dealing with foreign dignitaries, namely Elizabeth Montgomery, who was well-used to civic functions; and Marjorie and Truman Lloyd-Manning, both of whom were ardent supporters of the neighbourhood watch scheme. On the other hand, there was Winnie Waterman and Arlette Sargeant, who on the face of it were pleasant enough women but who had in the past proved to be rather dizzy and responsible for one or two hair raising WI calamities in their time. Still Elizabeth would no doubt keep a watchful eye on her ladies. The Major knew nothing of the two youngest members of the party, Michael and David. Their applications had stated they were waiting to go to university and would appreciate this once in a lifetime opportunity, however, the Major had heard rumblings on the grapevine that binge drinking and the hope that they were heading to Holland for a couple of days of recreational drug taking were in order, and decided to keep them under close scrutiny. Joyce and Arthur Whiplow, he felt were providing the 'common touch' as he liked to think of it – they ran the post office in Phoxton village. For political correctness the council had given a place to Wesley Singh owner of the VG shop on the road out of Flipping Bodbury. The Major had little knowledge of Mr Singh but had been very appreciative of his late opening hours on more than one occasion, and thus felt assured that a man of such high work ethics would be an asset to the group. The only other fly in the ointment that the Major had not anticipated was the late selection of Rodney Falstaff, a recently retired dentist. Generally well thought of in the area he had surprised his clients by retiring early and the town gossips were currently discussing the fact that Rodney had been suffering for years with narcolepsy, which his faithful dental nurse Shirley had been covering up largely due to the fact that she had three illegitimate children to support on her own, and also partly because she had a secret passion for Rodney. The Major had been amused to learn that many in the town had shunned Rodney recently because they had misunderstood his affliction and had believed him to be having sex with dead people. There it was then, the merry band of travellers that the Major would be chaperoning for the next five days; he wondered to himself if 25 years in the Light Infantry was sufficient training for such a task.

On a cold morning in March the group assembled in the car park of Hendersons Wine Bar, and the Major having dispensed with the necessary health and safety instructions, ticked off names on his clipboard and was noticeably edgy for a man used to commanding his troops. Elizabeth Montgomery had packed and repacked her carpet bag, a seasoned traveller she was not one to be weighed down by unnecessary baggage. She quickly positioned herself at the front of the coach and inspected her fellow travellers as they boarded. Elizabeth was amazed at the choice of Winnie and Arlette; they were fine as amateur fund raisers but hardly town ambassadors. She was also concerned that the two young boys on the trip were actually intent on turning it into a booze cruise or to gain life experience of perhaps a sexual nature. Winnie fumbled in her cavernous bag, as she struggled down the narrow coach aisle, and eventually produced several rustling packets.

"Wurther's Original anyone? Or my personal favourite a Foxy Glacier..." Winnie called out and catching up with Arlette she stumbled into her seat giggling away.

"I haven't been on a coach trip since I was a young girl," Arlette began to no one in particular and David and Michael the two youngest travellers who were sat at the back of the coach hastily turned up their iPods fearing that they had made a grave mistake by joining this trip.

Once on the motorway heading south the general level of banter increased and everyone was optimistic about the days ahead. The Major taking his responsibilities very seriously continuously checked his notes, and hastily hid his documentation whenever a member of the party approached him. Two hours into the journey and only 80 miles nearer to their destination they found themselves huddled on an embankment at the side of the motorway awaiting a replacement coach. A tyre blow out at 65 miles per hour had been an unfortunate calamity so soon into their travels. The noise of the traffic rushing past helped to mask the general chorus of profanities uttered when Winnie Waterman unhelpfully suggested a game of eye spy might help to pass the time. Not until Arlette slyly passed round her hip flask did the mood of the group begin to improve.

"I never travel without a wee dram," Arlette informed her fellow travellers, "purely medicinal you understand, just to settle the stomach when travelling. Drink up, plenty more to be had when we hit the duty free."

The Major's fruitless negotiations with the coach company were interrupted by Wesley Singh.

"Pardoning me Mr Major, but my brother-in-law runs a coach company in Luton, he can have a coach here for us in 30 minutes. I am hoping that will be helping you Mr Major." The Major breathed a sigh of relief and Wesley was given a round of applause and having everyone's undivided attention took the opportunity of giving out discount vouchers for his stores.

Having driven like the wind once on board the new coach, they managed to make up some time by foregoing a stop for lunch only to find that as they approached the port at Dover that due to industrial action on the part of the port authorities, there would be an estimated three hour delay in getting onto the ferry. Once more the group moaned and groaned and began to wonder at the sense in putting themselves forward for this trip, even if it was a freebie. Winnie, who had already been wedged inside the miniscule on-board toilet, decided not to risk a second attempt and headed off with Arlette and Elizabeth in search of larger toilets and nourishment. Having found both they then spent the next hour trying to find the right coach to get back onto. When they finally did so their fellow travellers were amazed that they had failed to notice that their coach was the only one in the queue plastered with Luton FC flags and banners on it, as it was ready for use on Saturday for their away match and had been the only replacement available to rescue them.

Arlette's medicinal stomach-settler proved to be quite the opposite for some members of the party during a very choppy channel crossing. The Major and Elizabeth appeared to be the only ones who did not turn green on the ferry and a subdued, ill looking group reassembled to continue their journey across northern Europe.

Several hours later, the first to step off the coach, the Major took it upon himself to check them all in to the Hotel. Leaving the weary travellers slumped in armchairs in the hotel lounge, tired, hungry and coach sick.

"Sorry to be the bearer of bad news chaps, but there appears to have been a little confusion over our booking – it seems we'll all have to share, but they have assured me that they are twin bedded and not doubles; you are in with me Elizabeth." The party looked at one another.

"I can't possibly share," said Elizabeth Montgomery affronted. "I need my own room. This simply isn't good enough Major; go back in at once and tell them who we are!" She was becoming quite hysterical at the thought of being the object of gossip rather than the one doing the gossiping.

"Don't worry my dear Elizabeth, it's only for the one night and it could be rather a hoot!!" the Major grinned.

"I simply..." Elizabeth Montgomery was ushered, still complaining towards the hotel.

An hour later, clutching her housecoat and Liberty print soap bag tightly to her bosom, she squeezed past the Major.

"If you don't mind I'll use the bathroom first." She pursed her lips as she turned on her heel making a great show of locking the door.

The party met for pre-dinner drinks in the bar before taking their seats for their evening meal. The Major banged his gavel on the table and called for the assembled group's attention, this took some time as a general holiday mood had taken hold and several drinks had been consumed in the bar before dinner. These had taken immediate effect as most of the travellers had left the contents of their stomachs in the English Channel.

"As you know tomorrow morning we commence the next leg of our journey to the proposed twin town. Can I remind you that we leave promptly at 8am and therefore I suggest an early night for everyone." This suggestion was met with a collective booing and the Major shuffled his paperwork and hastily sat down again.

"Vice bier dunkel!! If you please," Michael addressed the waiter, determined to fully immerse himself in the culture, he called upon his limited knowledge of German. David fell about laughing,

"What's on the menu – no doubt something with a very large sausage!"

"Now, now lads, a little decorum, there are ladies present." Major Ronaldson turned to Arlette for help, who sensing the Major had had enough for one day decided to take charge of the entertainment and keep an eye on the youngsters.

"Do either of you lads fancy joining us for a game of cards once dinner is over?" she asked. "Though I warn you, we play for money!"

"Absolutely, count us in," came the positive reply from the boys and Arlette winked at the Major as their main courses arrived.

Dinner passed with general mayhem and hilarity, and eventually stifling a yawn, the Major turned to Elizabeth. "Shall we turn in?"

Elizabeth Montgomery coloured as the rest of the party let out whoops and claps.

"You see Arthur, you're never too old, you only have to watch daytime chat shows to know that anything goes these days. There's all sorts of apparatus you can get to help you." Joyce's voice carried far louder when she had consumed a couple of glasses of wine and Arthur nearly choked on his crème caramel.

"Keep your voice down Joyce," Arthur retorted but it was too late.

"Well really." Elizabeth had caught Joyce and Arthur's exchange and stood up from the table, heading for her room, closely followed by Purple Ronnie (as he was affectionately now known by the group) with much puffing and blowing. They were closely followed by Marjorie and Truman Lloyd Manning. Marjorie had insisted, upon reaching the hotel, that Truman upgrade them to a suite on a different floor to the rest of the group to ensure she wasn't troubled by any rowdy behaviour.

Joyce was shuffling the cards as Arthur placed another schooner of beer on the table in front of the assembled group. In the corner of the lounge area Rodney was gently snoring once again. It had been decided early on that Wesley would keep a check on Rodney throughout the trip.

"Now who's in?" she asked the group. Arlette, Winnie, Michael and David took their seats, closely followed by Wesley who was reluctant to go to bed too early. Two hours and several games of peanuckle later, Michael piped up;

"I've got to say, I didn't know oldies could be such card sharks."

"Just because we are advanced in years, doesn't mean we don't know 'how to get down with the kids'," Joyce retorted.

"Right that's it. No television until after the watershed for you from now on, Joyce love." He laughed affectionately at his wife.

The following morning, the Major and Elisabeth made their way to breakfast bright eyed and bushy tailed which was more than could be said for the rest of the party; Wesley sloped off once the food arrived on the pretext of phoning home, but it was more to do with his colossal hangover than anything else. Rodney fell asleep at the table and Michael and David sat drinking vast mugs of black coffee whilst wearing their sunglasses.

"I rather think we are having the last laugh now don't you Major!" Elizabeth Montgomery sat smugly buttering her toast and ordering a fresh pot.

Once again the Major shepherded his flock onto the coach, ticking off on his register to ensure no-one was left behind. Major Ronaldson had spent much of the coach journey trying to inspire his fellow passengers with facts about the places they were passing through, however much of this fell on deaf ears apart from the rapt attention he received from Elizabeth. Despite the relentless miles of autobahns the party had driven through the spectacular scenery of Belgium and northern Germany, and he had pointed out to his weary companions the crossing of the Rhine, Elbe and Oder but to little avail. The highlight for the travellers appeared to be the pit-stops where Wesley Singh was constantly astounded by the price of everything, despite being repeatedly reminded about the power of the euro, and Winnie and Arlette had a never ending capacity to discuss the merits or lack of foreign toileting arrangements. The easiest member of the party was Rodney, who had slept for almost the entire day. Late afternoon had seen them cross the border into Poland and those with an inkling of geography realised their twin town must reside within this country. There had been some murmurings of discord due to the fact that Flipping Bodbury had recently seen an influx of cheap Polish labour however; the Major had quickly quelled the potential mutiny. Spirits were raised when they discovered that the second hotel was able to accommodate everyone without the need to double up again. Elizabeth Montgomery was secretly disappointed by this news. A far more subdued group assembled for dinner that evening and the older members of the party began to disperse to their rooms after the meal, lacking the energy of the previous night for revelry; much to the Major's relief.

"I always find a spot of suduko very relaxing," Elizabeth addressed David, whom she feared was surgically attached to his mobile phone, his fingers constantly tapping on the gadget. She handed him a tatty paper booklet of puzzles and a pencil which he received as if it were a stick of dynamite. As soon as she had left the room he dropped the book into a wastebin and returned to the important task of further updating his profile on Facebook.

The day of reckoning dawned and the travellers boarded the coach for the final leg of the outbound journey; delighted to be told a mere 40 minute trip would take them to their proposed twin town. As they approached what appeared to be a ghost town, devoid of people and prosperity, a stark contrast to their Cotswold idyll, they were aware that the dishevelled flags and bunting lining the streets reflected the condition of the town itself. Spirits dropped tangibly as they came to a halt in the town square, the centre piece of which was an unusually shaped obelisk reminding the younger travellers of a male member and provoking hysterics generally. The Major called for decorum as he stepped from the coach and assembled his group. In front of the obelisk stood two rotund, aficionados.

Next to them was a small child clutching a wilting posy and standing beneath a tatty banner claiming "Welcome to Schlopp."

The party stood open-mouthed, staring at what greeted them. The silence was broken by a lone off-key trumpeter and disappointment hung tangibly in the air.

"That just about sums it up!" Michael mumbled to David trying to retain some composure.

"How sensible of Rodney to be in the land of nod whilst we're in the land of drudge," replied David, heading back to the coach in disgust. "Mind you, they've been doing better than us in Eurovision so they must be doing something right."

"Oh really," sighed Elizabeth, who had been expecting a beautiful, rustic, historical town, "do you think they forgot to rebuild it after the war?"

A Developing Plan

Councillor Mervyn Harper reclined in his fake leather swivel chair with his feet on his desk, and pondered the proposal that had been put to him earlier that morning. Mervyn, a Liberal Democrat Councillor had achieved his position as Town Councillor for Flipping Bodbury and its neighbouring villages in the Cotswolds by default. His opponent Jack Stanbridge had committed political suicide by declaring a baby presented to him whilst out campaigning was an 'ugly little fellow' whilst within earshot of the Flipping Bodbury Gazette's political correspondent, and therefore this formerly staunch Conservative stronghold had suddenly been shaken up by a revolt against him. So Mervyn had won support on the back of this, but now in office and actually representing the area he was proving to be unpopular. Mervyn had been born and bred in the Cotswolds and had recently inherited a piece of land known as Bodbury Green to the far east of the town, which was generally used by the townsfolk to walk dogs, play football and for teenagers to congregate in order to drink illicit bottles of cider. Today however, Mervyn had met with Martin Townsend of Digbury

Homes who had offered him a vast amount of money to purchase the Green and build 25 new homes. This offer could not have arrived at a better time as Mervyn was dealing with the death duties from his mother's estate and had managed to run up a considerable debt of his own.

"Putting my cards on the table, Merv, basically you get planning permission for the site in place and I'll buy it for £500,000. I think you'll find it a very generous offer and worth a little input on your part." Martin Townsend had done his research on Mervyn, he knew that this was a low offer considering the potential for the land but he was shrewd enough to guess that it was life changing sum for Mervyn.

Unbeknownst to his constituents and Martin Townsend, Mervyn was an on-line gambler; he had come to gambling late in life. Mervyn would bet on anything from traditional horse-racing, bingo, the dogs and to the extremes of predicting the date of the first mating call of the bull-frog, for which he had won £500 by simply using Sheila's (his wife's) birthday. Mervyn had kidded himself for some considerable time that on-line gambling was not really gambling at all, as no physical money changed hands, however recently he had started to receive his credit card statements and had realised that his debts were spiralling out of control. So here today came salvation in the form of Digbury Homes property developers. During the meeting it had all sounded so straightforward, Mervyn needed to simply ensure that the planning permission was granted to develop the site with 25 new homes, to include some affordable housing, to keep in line with the government's targets, and then Martin Townsend would buy the land from Mervyn and all his problems would be solved. However, once alone again in his office Mervyn realised that he would have no particular influence on the planning office, and he was well aware that the townsfolk would put up considerable opposition to the proposal. This predicament would require some serious thinking. Mervyn therefore switched from reading the proposal to checking the riders for the 2.50pm at Kempton Park in order to clear his mind.

The next three weeks were spent surreptitiously wining and dining the members of the town planning committee. Mervyn fell short of actual bribery on the basis that he didn't have the financial wherewithal and also lacked the required nerve. Where he was able to exert influence however, was by negotiating with the editor of the Flipping Bodbury Gazette to run a favourable slant on the development in return for leaking secret council information over the next few weeks in order to ensure a scoop for the Gazette.

Sheila Harper, Mervyn's social climbing wife, had been the driving force behind his joining the council. As a Bank Manager's wife she felt she had a certain position of standing in the community but she sought out further status and had delighted at the pomp and ceremony which came with being part of the council. Now in her mid-fifties, Sheila had been compared to Edwina Curry as she looked at the time of her notorious affair with John Major. This comparison secretly thrilled Sheila who believed Edwina to have been a bit of a vamp, voluptuous and womanly, most of those making the comparison however, were unlikely to have been doing so in a flattering manner. The idea of Edwina the vamp was somewhat faintly ridiculous. Sheila threw herself into the role of councillor's consort and her requirement never to be seen in the same outfit twice at a council function only added to Mervyn's spiralling debts, of which she was blissfully unaware. At the first mention of selling the Green Sheila had spent the windfall in her head a hundred times over and pressure was therefore mounting on Mervyn to secure the deal.

Meanwhile planning notices had been posted on the trees and railings at the edge of the green and the residents had been swift to rise in protest. The first such protest meeting was held in the function room at the town hall, organised primarily by Patrick Sargeant, a retired History Professor whose home and garden adjoined the Green and who would therefore feel the impact most keenly. Patrick's wife, Arlette, a key member of the WI had produced protest leaflets which had been swiftly distributed by the WI ladies who were always quick to respond to a crisis. The townsfolk of Flipping Bodbury loved a get together of any type and the call to a protest meeting was met with a tremendous turnout. The leading players of the town were out in force, keen to protect this small corner of their town which had won prizes for its outstanding beauty and was a tourist hotspot.

Patrick called the meeting to order and introduced the various members of the action group which had been formed to lobby the town planners and formulate their opposition to the proposed development. Key players in the group were sat at a raised table; Major Ronaldson ex-Light Infantry and recently a leading figure in the town twinning committee, well respected and good friends with the Lord Lieutenant of the county. Alasdair Crossley, the tall dark and handsome owner of Crossley Hotels, a small family run chain of hotels whose flagship The Malmsbury Spa was situated just outside the town. Sitting next to Alasdair was Arlette Sargeant, Patrick's dotty but delightful wife and her partner in crime Winnie Waterman who was championing the humble dog walkers who used the Green for both exercising their dogs and meeting with likeminded individuals on a regular basis.

"Sorry to interrupt, Patrick," said a voice entering the hall, "but I've just seen Crispin Granger and his band of eBay warriors tying themselves to trees on the Green. I think they're forming a sit-in." Elizabeth Montgomery, lady Chair of the WI came marching up to the top table, her sensible shoes squeaking as she walked stoutly.

"Oh, God," muttered Patrick getting up, "we better see what that bunch of layabouts is up to before we go any further." He turned to the assembled residents. "There will be a slight delay whilst we investigate a report that eco warriors are currently erecting a camp on the Green." He paused briefly to persuade a couple of members of the team to accompany him and set off out of the town hall for the short walk to the Green.

Crispin Granger was a conservationist, or tree hugging layabout as Patrick liked to think of him. He had mustered together a small group of followers who were equally work shy and made their presence felt from time to time in the name of saving the planet. Patrick personally believed if they had a wash and got a job they would achieve a lot more than sitting watching day time TV all day and waiting for a reason to band together. He would have had more time for them if they ever left the safety of Flipping Bodbury and set off in the world to save the planet rather than sitting around talking about it.

Approaching the Green the committee members could see tents were being erected, and Crispin was climbing a ladder propped up against a decaying elm tree.

"I'm not sure this is a good idea Crispin," called out Winnie Waterman, "I don't think tying yourself to that branch will be very safe." She turned to Arlette Sargeant,

"I know for a fact he didn't get his knot tying badge in cubs, I do hope he's improved his reef knot since then."

"Now Crispin, it's very good of you to stage a protest but practically speaking I'm not sure this will be of much use." Patrick was trying to keep the irritation out of his voice because he knew he would be losing his audience back in the town hall if kept waiting too long. "Why don't you come to the meeting and we'll talk about what we can do collectively as a town?"

"We need action not leaflets Mr Sargeant; actions speak louder than words in these cases." Crispin shifted uncomfortably on his branch and continued wrapping rope around his waist. "These fascist developers think they can take every bit of our land for their own commercial gain, well they'll have to take me with it." At this rousing speech he overreached, and as he tried to grab hold of a higher branch it snapped away from him and he plummeted to the ground with a girly yell.

Everyone rushed forward and the WI ladies present were immediately intent on first aid, Patrick however, swiftly called 999 on his mobile, and murmured that his meeting would now be even later starting and something about bloody do-gooders was heard.

Having actually only fallen about ten feet Crispin did little actual harm to himself other than breaking a small bone in his foot but it was sufficient for him to claim it as an example of capitalists inflicting violence on the unsuspecting, which was nonsense but made him feel better about having simply fallen out of a tree less than five minutes into his protest. The meeting back at the town hall eventually began with a dwindled audience and little was achieved. Patrick was packing away his things as Jamie and Luke Henderson approached him.

"Wondered if you fancied a drink Patrick?" Jamie Henderson and his brother Luke ran Hendersons Wine Bar, and were as against the Green being built upon as everyone else. "We have a suggestion for getting this development stopped." Patrick was ready to listen to anything on offer and the three headed over to the wine bar.

"The way we see it, the only way to stop the development is by getting Mervyn to forget the whole idea and donate the Green to the town." Jamie handed Patrick a malt whiskey and looked at his brother conspiratorially.

"That would be perfect in an ideal world, but there is no way Mervyn is going to do that, why should he?"

Patrick immediately felt this was a waste of time.

"He might be persuaded to," chipped in Luke smiling.

"Now boys, much as I appreciate your help, I don't think we want to do anything against the law, or am I misunderstanding you both?" Patrick looked anxiously from one to the other and then around the bar to see who might be listening.

"Let's just say we may have a solution to this whole problem and you can rely on our discretion Patrick." Jamie answered.

Thanking the boys profusely for their offer of help, Patrick stated that his principles would only allow him to challenge the development through the proper channels, and much as he was tempted to swiftly put a stop to this stress and worry he couldn't partake in anything underhand. Jamie and Luke admired his honesty. Once Patrick had left the bar Jamie immediately turned to Luke.

"So we do it anyway, right?" he questioned his brother.

"Course we do, we can't have a nice bloke like Patrick worked up like this." Patrick had been a regular in the bar for years and had been a great friend of their father's so the boys felt duty bound to do something to help.

Tracey Cox had worked as a secretary for Mervyn at the bank for six months since leaving secretarial college. She enjoyed the work very much but working for 'Merv the Perv' as she called him was uncomfortable. Mervyn didn't actually sexually harass

Tracey but he made her feel uncomfortable with his comments about how she looked, and she could feel his eyes on her much of the time when she was working. Another regular at Hendersons bar, she was just ordering a gin and tonic after work on Friday evening whilst waiting for a friend to join her when.

"It's on the house, Tracey." Jamie smiled at her. "Wondered if I might join you for a drink and a chat?" Tracey's stunned face remained transfixed as he carried her drink round from the bar and directed her to one of the more secluded booths.

Some twenty minutes later, Tracey, completely unused to the attention of so attractive a male was putty in Jamie's hands. Having already ascertained that Tracey had no loyalty to Mervyn, Jamie explained to her what they needed her to do.

"Everyone has a weakness Tracey, and I wondered if you might be able to find Mervyn's weakness?" Jamie gave her the benefit of his most winning smile and the idea of this conspiratorial arrangement made Tracey's heart race. The Henderson brothers were easily the most glamorous men in the area and to be even partly associated with their elite social set would make Tracey the envy of her friends. And so several days later Tracey was back in Hendersons and toasting her success with champagne, the brother's new they had the information they needed.

Setting up a fictitious finance meeting with 'Merv the Perv', as the brother's now also referred to Mervyn, was easy and with Tracey's help photo static proof of Mervyn's gambling addiction, spiralling debts and erroneous expenses claims added up to quite a bit of ammunition.

"Good afternoon Jamie, Luke." Mervyn shook hands with the brother's as they entered his office under the premise of securing a bank loan. "How can I be of help to you today?"

"Actually Mervyn, it's more about what we can do for you," smirked Jamie.

For the next ten minutes Jamie regaled Mervyn of the details that Tracey had provided him with and as Mervyn squirmed and used words such as blackmail and espionage the brothers knew they were backing him into a corner.

"Think of it this way Mervyn, you could hand over the Green to the town as a gesture of goodwill and be seen as a remarkable citizen and councillor or we could go to Sheila and the council with the evidence of your seedy lifestyle, she'll probably divorce you and you would lose your job, home and status. What's the worst that could happen if you hand over the Green, Sheila will miss out on a spending spree, but let's face it, she'll get over it and I'm sure you can think of some creative excuse to get you out of it. You have two days to make a decision or we go public with this." At that the brothers got up and left the meeting. Mervyn was still gasping and swearing as they left the building.

The following week the Flipping Bodbury Gazette ran a front page article with the headline;

"Councillor Mervyn Harper, local benefactor with his wife Sheila, at the official handing over ceremony of the Green."

The picture of Mervyn and Sheila shaking hands

with the smiling town Mayor made a very appealing front page. Patrick reading his copy in the bar later that evening looked up at Jamie as he placed another whiskey in front of him.

"Nothing to do with you was it?" Patrick said with a smile that showed his gratitude.

"Don't know what you're talking about Patrick!" Jamie answered.

A Summer of Fates

The last morsel of chocolate Easter egg had barely been consumed when the ladies of the Flipping Bodbury WI gathered together in Winnie Waterman's orangery to discuss the forthcoming Summer Fete. This annual event, a stalwart of the WI calendar, involved weeks of planning and various spats along the way, and it had become the norm to hold the meetings on a Monday afternoon at the home of Winnie Waterman who, famous for her unusual nibbles and fast flowing refreshments, was a founding member of the towns WI. Although considerably ditsy in her day to day life, her heart was in the right place and her generosity knew no bounds.

"Ladies, I draw your attention to the first item on the agenda. No thank you Winnie, one glass of rum punch at this time of day is quite sufficient." Elizabeth Montgomery, Lady Chair of the WI, endeavoured to bring the chattering group to discuss the items on the agenda but as usual these gatherings were difficult to keep on track.

"Now, I believe our first point should be to decide

upon the date. I am aware that the cubs are using the village green the first Saturday in July as they are holding their annual camp. I understand that they can no longer use the field on Nason Farm due to that unfortunate incident with the neighbouring alpaca farm; still, thanks to lottery funding many of the tents that were destroyed in the rampage have now been replaced." General titters of amusement followed this last remark and Elizabeth tapped her biro on the coffee table for concentration to return. "This brings me to suggest the second Saturday that same month, which I feel is still early enough to avoid clashing with Crackerjacks Nursery Fun Day which is now taking place at the end of the month."

The meeting continued apace until the allocation of stalls was mentioned, at which point the usual infighting and territorial disputes arose and Elizabeth had to call the group to order once again.

"Marjorie, it is very kind of you to offer donkey rides and I feel sure that this will be a popular attraction with the children but can you be sure Malvolio will behave himself." Elizabeth had encountered the unruly donkey once before when he had escaped from his enclosure and had formed a very intimate relationship with one of the stone hogs outside Elizabeth's front porch. The memory of this desecration was still fresh in her mind.

"Don't worry Elizabeth. Malvolio should have finished his mating season by then and now he has his fancy head collar he is much more manageable." Marjorie Lloyd-Manning nonchalantly waved aside this concern. For many years Marjorie had seen herself as the lady of the manor living up at Phoxton Manor, and looking down upon the town from her lofty position, in both senses of the word. That is until the donkeys arrived. Four unruly beasts were quite literally dumped on her front lawn and after the initial shock had worn off and one of the donkeys had borne a foal, Marjorie became a reformed character and went so far as to rescue her four-legged squatters.

Elizabeth, remaining unconvinced but knowing how popular donkey rides would be reluctantly added them to her list of attractions and moved the meeting along. Thus were the wheels put in motion for this annual fundraising event.

On an uncommonly gorgeous summer's day the Fete Committee recruits began to assemble on the Green to prepare for the big event. As bunting was strung from the trees and marquees erected, by the more physically able, the Green began to flourish. Major Ronaldson had managed to enlist the help of the cub scouts with painting the picket fence that bordered the entire perimeter, and although there had been much white paint spilled it had generally been a successful endeavour, and the cubs were rewarded with their DIY badge; along with plentiful supplies of refreshments. Flipping Bodbury looked at its best in the sunshine, the quintessential English town. The Green was beautifully mown with diagonal stripes, with a babbling brook running through the main street and the obligatory eccentric residents out in force to boot.

Elizabeth Montgomery, clip board always at hand, was marshalling her troops with gusto.

"Now, you have all been allocated to a team to do

specific tasks, I trust everyone remembers which team they are in. Major Ronaldson will be overseeing the collection of tables from the Church Hall; the marquees are already in place so the next job is to begin setting up the stalls. You have your jobs ladies, let's get to it." Elizabeth waved them all onwards and headed over to interfere with Marjorie Lloyd-Manning, who was attempting to direct a reversing horse box, driven by her husband, Truman, onto the Green.

"Left hand down a bit Truman, come on there's plenty of room, just keep going." Marjorie was gesticulating madly at her husband who was managing admirably whilst completely ignoring his wife's instructions.

"There, I think this is an excellent spot for you Marjorie, plenty of shade for the donkeys, and a good open space to walk them up and down. Now you are sure that Malvolio won't misbehave aren't you." Elizabeth looked at Marjorie over her glasses with a worried expression.

"Malvolio is a tamed beast these days Elizabeth, you can rely on that." This was said with more conviction than she really felt, but after all how much trouble could a donkey cause at a summer fete? Marjorie comforted herself with the fact that her niece, Portia, would be in charge of Malvolvio; the pair had formed a committed bond in the months since Marjorie and Portia had rescued them.

At the far right hand corner of the Green the magnificent oak tree stood as an ancient protector watching over them. Beneath its enormous bows, protected from the sun, the Brownie pack was doing a roaring trade in temporary tattoos for 20p. Elizabeth Montgomery felt it was time to wander over and give the girls some encouragement. Charlie Brown, a precocious eight year old whose parents were obviously post the Snoopy generation, was busily applying the said tattoos as she approached.

"Well then Charlie, how are we doing?" Elizabeth peered closer in order to get a better view of the vaguely familiar shape forming on a small child's arm as Charlie was sponging the back off the tattoo.

"It's very popular, we are making a killing!" Elizabeth winced at the terminology and Charlie continued to carefully remove the backing from the tattoo and looked up at Elizabeth's now horrified face. The image revealed was that of a pentogram, perfectly formed on the arm of a very pleased small girl.

"Where did you get the tattoos from Charlie?" Elizabeth asked as panic was rising in her voice.

"My brother bought them from the Sunday market at Little Chadbury, he goes there every week because it's where the Hell's Angels meet. He said these were all spares so I could have them." Charlie looked very pleased with herself but Elizabeth was becoming more and more visibly distressed as she examined the contents of the tub of tattoos finding CND symbols, skull and crossbows and gender logos galore. She dropped her cavernous shoulder bag onto the table and having rummaged through the contents pulled out a bottle of Max Factor 'Perfectly Rose' nail polish and presented it to Charlie.

"I think we'll diversify and offer nail painting

instead Charlie." Elizabeth thrust the bottle at the girl whilst grabbing the tub of tattoos with her other hand. "I'll take these and you can return them to your brother later." With that she turned on her heels and hastily made her way towards the refreshments tent to fortify her nerves with a large glass of Pimms.

Not far from the beer tent Drew and Blair Bantham set about displaying their selection of books on the second-hand book stall. As joint owners of 'The Cock and Bull Story Bookshop', the pair were always on hand to get their wares out for a good cause.

"Prop the signed copy of 'Living it Large' at the front Drew, we want as many people as possible to see it; it could be our most profitable sale." Blair passed the book to Drew, who was easily distracted with all that was going on around them. "I'm not really sure about these ones, I mean how many of the WI ducks would admit to buying 'Preserves – a Beginners Guide'!" Drew laughed and carried on his favourite pastime of people spotting.

"This is going to be so much fun, you can learn a lot about the locals from what they buy, their choice of book speaks volumes – pardon the pun! Oh I can't wait to see who is opening the Fete." He returned to gawping at the comings and goings and Blair busied himself stacking the trestle table only pausing at the approach of their friends Winnie and Arlette.

"Do we know if the Mayor is the official ribbon cutter today, only I was hoping for an A list celeb and Drew says there's no chance of that?" Blair brandishing a copy of 'Men are From Mars, Women are from Venus' thrust the book at Winnie who was a sucker for self-help books of any type.

"Haven't you heard?" Winnie was nearly apoplectic, "You of all people, I thought you would be the first to know?"

"What?" Blair squealed, hopping from foot to foot and distraught at not knowing a piece of gossip first. "Tell, tell, immediately," he demanded.

"Well, they've only gone and got your one true God of the seventies." Winnie was deliberately toying with him.

"Winnie Waterman put poor Blair out of his misery. It is now clear to us that he has lost the monopoly on village gossip and will forever have to bow to our greater knowledge," Arlette took up the teasing.

"Jon Hinman." Winnie simply uttered the name. Blair looked about to faint and Drew finally decided to pay attention.

"Do you actually mean that the Lord Jon Hinman will be here in a matter of minutes as the aficionado of our humble village fete?" Drew knew that this could prove to be a remarkable day for his partner Blair who adored all things Hinman.

The loud speaker crackled and hissed to life as Elizabeth Montgomery adjusted her cue cards and raised her shoulders.

"Ladies and gentlemen, boys and girls, and dignified guests," she began in her most impressive public speaking voice, and glancing sideways to receive approval from Major Ronaldson, her beau. "What a wonderful turnout for this our annual Summer Fete and aren't we lucky with the weather this year." This received general nods of agreement and much here-hereing from the audience who were largely awaiting the official opening in order that they could return to the beer tent, or in the case of the children waste more money on pointless purchases.

"It gives me great pleasure to hand you over to our special guest who has kindly agreed to officially opening today's proceedings. Mr Jon Hinman." Elizabeth graciously beckoned him onto the centre of the makeshift stage.

"It is lovely to be here, I love a good Fete and in the sunshine too it all looks delightful." He waved his arms about him in an extravagant gesture. "I now declare this Fete well and truly open." With a flourish he cut the red ribbon in front of him and everyone clapped and cheered. From the back of the crowd there was a commotion as Blair Bantham was hastily trying to get to the front, he dashed forward just as the Lord Jon Hinman was waving the scissors in the air with one hand and royally waving with the other. Having misjudged the distance, as in his vanity he was not wearing his glasses, Blair cannoned into the front of the makeshift stage and the Lord Jon Hinman wobbled precariously and fell forwards, as if diving into the crowd at a rock concert. Fortunately Drew sensing disaster looming, had been right behind Blair and was able to use his six foot frame to its best advantage and magnificently caught the Lord Jon Hinman in his arms, and gracefully placed him on the ground.

"Oh my Lord!" cried Blair, not inappropriately.

"What a hero you are Drew, that was simply incredible." Blair was a blithering wreck, but his interest in the Lord Jon Hinman had been completely overshadowed by the heroic performance of his partner.

Elizabeth Montgomery having nearly died of apoplexy while this whole debacle had been going on, now stood beside Mr Hinman and was frantically apologising and brushing his clothing down.

"My dear Elizabeth," the Lord Jon Hinman reassured her, "that is the most fun I have had in a very long time, now if you'll excuse me I must thank my rescuer." He turned to Drew who was being worshipped by Blair and the three of them headed off for Pimms, making this one of the happiest days of Blair's life.

Portia Lloyd-Manning stroked the nose of the wayward donkey she had tethered beside her and received a friendly nudge of encouragement in return. Malvolio was Portia's favourite of the rescued donkeys mainly because she could identify with his plight and his eagerness to follow his own path. Portia, daughter of Miles and Jennifer Lloyd-Manning, knew all about being passed from one place to another. Her parents, as committed aid workers, were faultless in their devotion to a suffering human cause but were not so devoted to a 15 year old girl left behind at boarding school, or dumped on her aunt and uncle during the holidays. Prior to starting school Portia had been dragged to every war torn corner of the world; wherever disaster struck her parents were quickly on the scene. However, when it became more difficult to lug a reluctant five year old around with them they quickly decided a good education was the answer and packed her off to St Catherine's school. Portia struggled at first with being kept in one place but quickly found her true vocation in life when she was introduced to the school's small animal compound. Here she really found her feet and it soon became evident that her goal in life was to become a vet.

Malvolio was becoming increasingly bored of being tied to a tree whilst all the other donkeys were paraded up and down the Green with wriggling and squealing children on their backs, he wanted very much to be a part of the action.

"I don't think so young man," Portia told him, sensing his unrest. "The last time you gave rides you took off across the cricket pitch and wrecked Mrs Banbury's herbaceous borders. Not to mention hospitalising poor little Johnny Moncton. You are staying firmly by my side today." Portia stroked his neck, feeling sorry for the naughty donkey, but knowing chaos followed his every move.

At age 15 Portia was a late developer, more interested in animals than fashion and beauty. She was only just beginning to gain an interest in the male species and on this particular day she was on the lookout for a glimpse of the famous Henderson brothers, who she heard were the ultimate example of the male species. Leaving Malvolio and the other donkeys in what she believed to be the capable hands of the girl guides that were assisting her with the donkey rides, Portia headed over to the plant stall to extrapolate yet more pocket money from her aunt in order to try her luck in Hendersons Beer tent.

Malvolio was always quick to sniff out disinterest and incompetence in his guards, and had swiftly begun to nibble at the rope that was tethering him to the oak tree. Sonia Garrett and Letitia Swain were far more interested in adjusting the hemline length of their guide uniforms and plumping up their inflatable bras to notice the malevolent donkey up to his tricks, and once satisfied that their new improved look would be sufficient to attract the nearby army cadets who were busily running the target shooting stand they neglected their post and wandered over to gain an introduction into all things military.

Having chewed a significant amount of rope, Malvolio gave one swift tug and was as free as a bird; he set off in pursuit of the smell of freshly baked cakes which was coming from the WI ladies 'Bake Off' tent. With the hullabaloo of the fete in full swing and a record turnout due to the fantastic weather, no one paid much attention to Malvolio plodding around the edge of the Green and he reached the rear of the 'Bake Off' tent unhindered. For a donkey that is an expert in escapology it was a mere matter of a quick tug on the canvas ties at the back of the tent to allow him access to the bounty that lay before him. At the precise moment of his arrival in the tent the WI ladies and the judging panel had assembled outside the tent in order to hear the announcements over the loud speaker and for the winners to receive their rosettes. Sometime later, Malvolio, a sweet-toothed donkey, had made short work of the vast array of buns, sponges and assorted cup-cakes on offer. The sponge itself had proved to be a donkey favourite but what Malvolio had not allowed for was the disconcerting effect on his belly that was caused by the large amount of butter icing he had ingested. A donkey with tummy ache is not a happy donkey and as he began to lurch forward towards the entrance to the tent the judges and dignitaries approached to put the rosettes on the winner's exhibits. Malvolios stomach made a very large rumble of protest just as the Mayor and his wife entered the cool darkness of the tent from the brilliant sunshine outside, and as their eyes adjusted to the dim light they were confronted with the melee before them. Gone was the vast array of beautifully presented cakes of every type imaginable, what remained resembled the aftermath of a food fight, cake stands knocked over, crumbled chunks of sponge strewn all over the floor and plates smashed to smithereens.

Malvolio was writhing in pain on the floor, his legs thrashing uncontrollably. He was desperately struggling to get onto his feet and had manoeuvred his body around so that his rear was now clearly on display to the crowd forming at the entrance to the tent. Loud high pitch sounds were emanating from Malvolios gut.

"Oh my goodness!" yelled Arlette quickly assessing the situation. "Grab that animal and call the vet." But just as she pushed Winnie towards Malvolio's head to steady him, he let out an almighty blast of flatulence and splattered the poor unsuspecting Mayor and his lady wife who became the recipients of his bowel contents.

Arlette pushed the Mayor and his wife aside as Malvolio lunged forward, his front legs buckling underneath him.

At this precise moment Portia, having been refused alcohol by Luke Henderson and palmed off with a ginger beer, was on her way to the cake tent to see if her aunt had won her usual first prize. She saw the commotion and turned immediately in the direction of the great Oak tree, Malvolio was no longer tethered to the tree and people were screaming inside the cake tent which could only mean one thing. Donkey trouble again. Portia pushed through the crowd who were trying to mop down the Mayor and his wife who was still clutching a bouquet, presented for opening the Fete, that now looked like a bowl of minestrone soup had landed on it. Upon seeing a writhing Malvolio, Portia shouted for the crowd to move back, quickly dialled the vet on her mobile, whilst angrily swearing at the WI ladies who were repeatedly calling for "that brute to be put down."

"Portia, calm down, Kieran, will be here any minute; he'll know what to do." Marjorie Lloyd-Truman, the most unlikely donkey supporter that ever lived was desperately trying to hide her concern about Malvolio's state from her niece who was clearly distraught.

Kieran Sadler, the Town's dependable vet, was already in attendance at the Fete. The RSPCA had been called to attend to the rats that were in distress from the 'Splat the Rat' stall where the participants, mainly the scouts, were actually trying to hit live rats with rounders bats. This was because Major Ronaldson, who was running the stall, had misunderstood the whole premise of the game. His grand-daughter, Lila-Belle on arrival at the stall was horrified, and having recently adopted a new-found animal rights conviction set the rats free. Further mayhem ensued as eight white rats had then to be rounded up by a rather large RSPCA lady who was already struggling with the heat of the day. Major Ronaldson, always the gentleman, offered the scouts one pound per rat retrieved, and soon they were being checked over by Kieran and boxed up to be despatched with the very grateful RSPCA lady to a rehoming centre. After this exhausting interlude Keiran was heading towards the beer tent when his phone rang with Portia hysterically yelling for him to help Malvolio.

Black bag in hand Kieran shooed away the disgruntled WI ladies who were still baying for blood. Malvolio's eyes were rolling and his mouth was frothing furiously as Kieran felt around his belly, whilst Malvolio was rolling from side to side with his legs flailing.

"Please move aside ladies, when we've seen to Malvolio we can sort out the rest of the mess." The cool calmness of authority dispersed the bakers who were ushered over to the beer tent for nerve steadying brandies by Truman, leaving his wife to look after Portia and Malvolio. Kieran having felt Malvolio's distended belly and checked his vital signs decided to wrestle the moaning donkey to his feet in order to try and alleviate the discomfort, and perhaps dislodge the flatulent colic that was causing his pain. Keiran knew that Portia feared that Malvolio had strangulated colic or more commonly known as a twisted gut but he actually felt the cause was more likely simple over indulgence in butter icing.

"Let's see if we can lead him round the Green and

gently work away some of the pain in his stomach by movement, he'll pass more gas and eventually disperse the butter mixture and it will gently ease. I'll give him a shot of Metacam to help with the griping but nature will take its course." Kieran looked at the relief on Portia's face as she began to register the fact that Malvolio was going to be alright. Smacking him firmly on his hind quarters she tried to make him move.

"Greedy pig!" she yelled at him, relief sweeping over her. "Look at the trouble you've caused again." But Malvolio firmly resisted all attempts to make him move. She moved round to hold Malvolio's neck, and gently rubbed his ears. As he struggled to his feet, pushed and pulled by Keiran and Portia his backend continually erupted and he gradually shook less. However, no amount of tugging could get him to move.

"I know what's wrong," Portia informed the vet, "He's been sulking all day because he wasn't allowed to give rides. If we could just put some small child on his back he'd feel like he was part of the Fete." Kieran sceptical of Portia's idea, decided it was worth a try as the animal needed to get moving. Grabbing the nearest small cub he could find he swung him up onto Malvolio's broad back and using a scarf, provided by Marjorie as a temporary leading reign they slowly moved forward out of the tent. Despite the upset and the wrecked cakes, the WI ladies being a benevolent bunch, forgave his misdemeanours and gently encouraged the subdued donkey to take some tentative steps to work off the ache in his stomach. Portia proudly led her mischievous ward making a mental note to have a word with her useless Girl Guide helpers when she found them.

Stepping down from her battered old jeep; Janey Davenport picked up her camera bag and throwing her satchel over her arm, sauntered nonchalantly through the fete, stopping every so often to make notes, or take the odd photograph. Her main purpose was sussing out Hendersons beer tent, where her former boyfriend, Luke would undoubtedly be holding court.

Having been 'sent to Coventry', or in this case the Cotswolds, to cover the summer fete, Janey was beginning to tire of her bosses punishment for her missed deadlines, and consistent lateness; he had been dishing out the most mundane and tedious covers for the last month now and it was starting to take its toll. However, the opportunity to see the man who had not only stolen her heart, but had humiliated her when he was caught in not too favourable circumstances with a colleague at the newspaper three years earlier, was too much to resist.

Passing countless stalls, offering homemade produce, raffle tickets for bric-a-brac prizes and a tombola, Janey was amused to see the dentist offering 'Teeth Whitening – within the hour!' Looking at the average age of those attending the fete, they could easily leave their sets with him and collect them later she thought, with a giggle. She was further amused by the fact that despite holding a newspaper, he appeared to be asleep under the panama hat he was wearing. Further along a rather beautiful woman was drawing caricatures and pencil portraits for what seemed to be an inordinately long queue – Julia Wainsford the local artist whose talent and confidence had grown since moving to the village, had attracted a large crowd, mostly young males, and not just for her ability to draw! Nearing the tent she could see Luke putting out a clapperboard sign advertising a special offer promotional drink. He was wearing faded cut off denims and a loose fitting shirt which only seemed to emphasise his tanned beauty – annoyingly her heart lurched.

Diverting round to the rear of the tent, Janey was intrigued by the array of brightly coloured bottles that were stacked several crates high on a small flat bed truck, partially covered by a tarpaulin. Her reporter's instinct was telling her to have a closer look. Walking back round to the front she studied the sign that advertised 'Absinhte – try it here first at Hendersons, sponsored by 'Wax Lyrical Beauty Salon'. "Sounds about right for you, Luke, it couldn't be anything other than, hot totty, sponsorship could it," she thought to herself. Luke looked up from hammering in the tent pegs, puce in the face from his exertions, but none the less handsome.

"Janey, how delightful," he stammered, "you must come and have a free one on us." Jamie, dropped the crate he was carrying and linking her arm, frogmarched her to the temporary bar whilst doing some quick thinking. Janey the journalist with a grudge against his brother was not a person he had wanted to see today of all days when he was palming off some of the fake booze that his younger brother had stupidly bought whilst on a drunken booze cruise with some ex-squaddies.

"Actually I think I've had quite enough free ones

from your rather energetic brother, thank you." She replied removing her arm from his grasp.

"Now don't be like that Janey, you and I always used to get on. Come and try the latest craze to hit the UK, it's going down a storm." Jamie poured the bright green liquid into a shot glass.

'I tried "Absinthe' in St Trop, and as I'm working today I think I'll pass thank you," she retorted, reaching into her bag for her notebook.

"All work and no play makes Janey a very dull reporter," Jamie mocked just as Janey took the empty bottle from him.

"Hold on a minute." Janey carefully studied the label on the bottle. "Where did you get this from? Absinthe is spelled with a th not ht, this is knock off isn't it?" She looked at him with a wry smile.

Out of the corner of his eye Jamie caught sight of Luke going to the truck behind the tent.

"Wait here one sec, I know Luke will be thrilled to see you." He rapidly pushed her into a vacant seat, handed her the drink and dashed out the back to Luke. Once he had quickly filled him in on their current predicament and reminded him that a controversial article in the local paper by Janey could ruin their chances of increasing their AA rating that was currently being reviewed, Jamie shoved Luke back into the tent to salvage the situation.

"Janey, hi, you look fantastic. About what happened Janey, I still feel terrible about Miranda and she turned out to be a real nightmare, not like you angel." He droned on with his usual line of patter and

Janey could feel the charm offensive beginning to work, largely because she really liked his charm!

"Let me make amends, what are you doing this summer, I've been offered a couple of weeks sailing in Dartmouth, might even take in the Regatta, how about joining us, just the old crowd, how about it?" Janey was beginning to feel her ability to resist disappearing and it would certainly beat more summer fete assignments. Perhaps she could overlook the fake booze and put her journalist nature on hold whilst she had a decent holiday.

"I'll leave you two to it, lots to do." Breathing a sigh of relief that another Luke disaster had been avoided, Jamie disappeared through the back of the tent amidst much clanking of bottles.

Later that day after the last of the union jack bunting was being taken down and the brownies had finished their meticulous search of the Green collecting any further stray rubbish, Elizabeth Montgomery and Major Ronaldson set out to dine at Hendersons Wine bar and reflect on the events of the day. From escaping rats and donkeys, to free-falling gay icons it had certainly been eventful and to cap it all, a great deal of money had been raised for a worthy cause. The charity of choice this year had been the 'Upper Modbury Displaced Beavers', another one of Winnie Waterman's bizarre but nevertheless necessary endeavours. The re-routing of the River Byford to prevent flooding in Upper Modbury village had been essential but its casualties, the beavers, were now currently being cared for temporarily at a nearby small animal sanctuary, soon to be joined by eight white rats...

A Wedding to Remember

Olivia Beckwith gazed out of the beautiful original sash window at the lake and distant fields, which was the view from her office in The Malmsbury Spa Hotel. This glorious part of the southern Cotswolds was drenched in early summer sunshine and she longed to be outside enjoying a rare warm day. The meeting was going on interminably. This was yet another planning session for the Cardew wedding in one month's time. The mother of the bride, Faye Cardew, and the mother of the groom, Veronica Whelps, were discussing in minute detail the positioning of the tables in the Cavanaugh Room where the reception was to be held. Tracey Jones, temporary help drafted in after it became clear that this particular wedding was taking over Olivia's entire work time was now sat, totally absorbed in wedding fever. Tracey had arrived on her first day at work with her Filofax in immaculately manicured hands, a neat blonde bob and petite pretty features and Olivia had feared the worst. However, Tracey had proved to be a gem. She had an ability to absorb hours of wedding drivel with an un-quenching thirst for more. She was a hit with Faye and Veronica because she was so enthusiastic, but Tracey was simply a wedding fetishist, she would never tire of consulting wedding magazines and websites. Olivia returned her full attention to the discussion and briefly caught the bride's eye, Emily Cardew look as uncomfortable as ever. The wedding of Emily Cardew and Charles Whelps was turning out to be the social event of the year, if not the decade, in this part of the Cotswolds. However, the bride-to-be did not appear to be as enthusiastic a member of the organising party as Olivia was accustomed to.

Olivia Beckwith had joined The Crossley Hotel chain four years previously and worked as Events Organiser at The Malmsbury Spa Hotel in Phoxton, a small village in the Cotswolds. Olivia had been at school with Miranda Crossley, who now co-owned the hotel chain with her brother Alasdair. Miranda and Olivia had lost touch after school, but had been reacquainted at a school reunion where Miranda discovered that Olivia had spent the intervening years at university studying events management and promptly interviewed her for the hotel at Phoxton. During the years that had followed her arrival at the hotel, Olivia organised various functions but the planning for the Cardew Wedding was beginning to take its toll on her and Olivia couldn't help but feel that Emily's heart wasn't really in this huge wedding extravaganza, which certainly was the most lavish that Olivia had seen to date. She couldn't deny however, that Emily was absolutely desperate to marry Charles, as she had seen the tenderness that existed between them. It appeared to be the mothers who were hell bent on a society wedding.

"I believe taffeta napkins would certainly fit in with our theme, so luxurious Faye." Veronica Whelps caressed the sample napkin as if it was a precious object and Olivia wondered for the hundredth time if she would ever see the end of this planning meeting.

"Taffeta is just the most elegant," began Tracey, unwittingly leading into another ten minute debate but fortunately Emily yawned purposely and her mother intervened,

"Perhaps we should carry on at home Veronica; we can have some tea and discuss it there." Faye looked in Olivia's direction and raised her eyebrows to indicate that she too felt that enough time had been taken up for one day, and she began to gather her belongings.

"Tracey will get the revised seating plan drawn up and email it to you all, and then I suggest we get together next week to go through any further changes and to clarify the positioning of the flowers in the room." Olivia stood and collected her papers, and to show that she really was finishing the meeting, she moved to the door.

Having closed the door Olivia could still hear Veronica and Faye in full sway.

"I find this whole wedding very draining." Olivia wandered back to her desk and Tracey collected together her samples and notes.

"I think it will be spectacular and Emily will have the best day of her life!" announced Tracey in her romantic trancelike state.

Olivia failed to find the enthusiasm for any more wedding talk and she decided to type up her notes from the meeting, before heading off to a well-earned tea break. In doing so she couldn't help but revisit the idea that Emily was being carried along on a path of organisation that she couldn't get off, and she was becoming completely swamped by her mother's overbearing nature and not particularly helped by her mother in law to be either. Not for the first time she wondered whatever the women would find to do with themselves when the big day was over.

During the next weekly management meeting Olivia gave an overview of the events in the pipeline. Alasdair Crossley always kept abreast of what was happening at The Malmsbury because not only was it his favourite hotel in the chain, being set in his beloved Cotswolds, but also because he and his sister both had private apartments there.

"The Cardew wedding is important to us Olivia, I understand that it is full-time commitment at the moment but this is a high spend wedding and in a recession we need to make sure we hold onto clients like these." Alasdair was also very well acquainted with the two families as they had been friends with his parents and he had been at school with Charles Whelps. "Is everything in order for their drinks party next week?" he directed his question at Olivia.

"We are just waiting confirmation of numbers, but otherwise we are completely ready." Olivia was aware that Alasdair and Miranda had been invited to the drinks party and she was leaving nothing to chance with the arrangements.

The following week a glorious late June evening provided the perfect temperature for the drinks party, which took place on the terrace at the back of the hotel overlooking the sweeping, layered, lawns down to the lake. The boathouse, newly painted and set beneath a centuries old weeping willow, provided the perfect romantic setting for photographers in search of wedding photo ambience. Olivia mingled with the select few guests and as usual, the parents of the bride and those of the groom were holding court. Again Olivia was aware of the overwhelming connection between Charles and Emily but this was overshadowed by their respective parents' desire for a socially acceptable event.

"As I was saying to Charles this morning, the Fortesque's only warranted a half page in Cotswold Life Magazine, I fully expect several paparazzi to be covering your wedding, you are a celebrity after all Charles." Veronica Whelps turned to Major Ronaldson, a long-time family friend who was accompanied by his granddaughter Lila Belle. Charles and Emily took the opportunity to wander away to talk to younger members of the gathering before Charles's mother could embarrass him further.

Secretly Charles would have preferred to simply whisk Emily off to some golden beach and have a wedding with just the two of them and absolutely no fuss, but Emily, whilst agreeing in principal, felt that they couldn't do that to either of their mothers' if they ever wanted to be able to speak to them again. She had persuaded Charles to go along with the big wedding idea and he had promised to bite his tongue and keep the peace for the sake of his beautiful bride to be. However, the thought of being forever excommunicated by his mother-in-law to be was at times irresistible. Charles Whelps was in fact a minor celebrity, having been recently cast in the role of Hamlet at the RSC in Stratford upon Avon and having received rave reviews, to his mother's delight and never ending boasting to the WI. From school plays he had found a desire to act and had followed his Rada training with taking every small part offered to him all over the country, whilst moonlighting as a jouster at Warwick Castle re-enactments every spare moment he had, until finally his persistence had paid off and he had landed the leading role. Veronica Whelps clearly felt she was now in the presence of the next Olivier and was fast outdoing Faye Cardew with invitations to prestigious local events due to her now infamous connections.

Olivia sort out Charles and Emily, with a view to reassuring herself that all was well and was met with a determined grimace from Charles.

"Beware of my mother, she's name-dropping from a great height and boring everyone on the minute detail of my fellow cast members." Charles, clearly embarrassed took another large swig of his Pimms, "I'm off to the bar to get a proper drink." He kissed Emily on the top of her head and headed off inside.

"This is all becoming quite a strain for Charles." Emily stated exactly what Olivia was thinking.

"That's not unusual at this stage of the proceedings," Olivia reassured her, "but I think it's really important to remember why you are doing this and try not to let it get on top of you both." She actually felt that the intense pressure of this wedding would not come between this pair, but could potentially affect their future relationships with their parents'; she had seen that happen before.

Wandering over to check the buffet that was being laid out Olivia overheard Elizabeth Montgomery, Lady Chair of the Phoxton WI,

"I was only remarking to my Tarquin the other day, that weddings have become a very casual affair these days to my mind, personally I prefer a Church service followed by a hotel reception, but they seem to grant licences for any old place. It won't be long before you can get married in Phoxton village hall, can you imagine that." She looked at Major Ronaldson to whom she was speaking but he had clearly been thinking of something else entirely as his response was wholly inappropriate. Olivia was of a mind to say that as Tarquin, her only child, so obviously batted for the wrong team it was more than likely that she would be attending a civil partnership service in the future, and she smiled to herself as she wondered how that would be viewed.

The gentle chink of metal on glass intimated that everyone's attention was required. Bradley Whelps was about to propose a toast to the soon to be happy couple,

"Dear friends, and soon to be extended family members, I just wanted to say a few words," and he continued to waffle on for the next five minutes on the joining of two great families which seemed to Olivia more an opening speech for Henry V than a toast at an intimate drinks party. The evening wore on and both families inter-mingled happily but Olivia noticed that Charles and Emily were the first to leave.

Several meetings took place over the next three weeks leading up to the big day itself and Olivia was concerned about how the interference of the two matriarchs was affecting Emily. Charles, being at rehearsals in Stratford, was able to escape most of these meetings. Olivia was also surprised by Bradley Whelps frequent appearance and seeming interest in all things floral. Faye's husband, Gerald, also arrived periodically to discuss the finer details of the place settings and by the time the final rehearsal took place Olivia felt as though her entire life had become enveloped in the Whelps / Cardew wedding. When she voiced her concerns to Tracey however, Tracey casually remarked how interesting it was that the parent's of the bride and groom were getting on like a house on fire, and wasn't that lovely. Olivia thought no more about it but turned her attentions to other events. She was currently ensconced in organising the WI's latest fundraising event, a fashion show to be held in the Lincoln Ballroom, complete with cat walk and lighting. Elizabeth Montgomery had handed the task over to Winnie Waterman and Arlette Sargeant, two devoted WI members and ardent fundraisers who were always on the lookout for an interesting cause. This particular event was to raise money for homeless transvestites which for some reason Elizabeth, who was blissfully unaware of the world around her, had assumed was something to do with the protection of bats in the wild. Olivia decided not to enlighten her and it was proving to be her favourite event of the year so far. The last time that Winnie and Arlette had organised an event of this nature they had hired Racey Stacey who did unusual magic tricks which largely consisted of firing ping pong balls out of several orifices but it had gone down a storm with all the husbands who had been dragged along to another boring WI event.

On the eve of the Cardew wedding, Olivia was working late at the hotel to ensure that everything was ready for the following day. Several of the couples family and close friends had already arrived at the hotel and were making a weekend of the event. Olivia feared for the weather, June had been glorious but moving into July the rain had begun and the forecast for the next day was more down pours. Fortunately, The Malmsbury Spa Hotel was equally spectacular inside as the beautiful setting outside. The hotel, built from traditional Cotswold stone, was grand and imposing and the entrance hall and huge sweeping staircase made the perfect indoor setting for photographs. Passing the dining room Olivia glanced at the Cardew party, and immediately noticed that even though Charles's protective arm was around her shoulders, Emily looked strained and pale. Turning back towards her office Tracey came running along the corridor the other way. The last thing Olivia wanted was more problems, she had had a late night previously attending and overseeing the WI charity fashion show, which had been a roaring success. Elizabeth Montgomery had been visibly dumbstruck when she realised who her WI were raising money for, but by the time they reached the finale, which was a stunning cabaret by the Lady Boys of Gloucestershire, even she was caterwauling and cheering them on. A great deal of money had been raised; everyone agreed it had been another triumph by Winnie and Arlette, if a little unconventional for the WI.

"I've checked the room one last time, everything is

in place for the ceremony in the Chester Room and they are just laying up the tables in the Cavanagh for the reception. If you don't mind I might just go now." Tracey looked a little flushed and uncomfortable as she gathered her things together.

"Thanks Tracey, I don't know what I'd have done without you these past few weeks, I'm sorry it's been so late tonight, once this wedding is over tomorrow we might calm down a bit." Olivia had enjoyed working with Tracey and her wedding enthusiasm had proved to be a godsend.

As feared the next day brought more rain and the inevitable last minute problems that were as much a part of wedding planning as the dress and cake. When Olivia arrived at work that morning a letter had been pushed under her office door. Dropping her belongings on the settee she quickly opened the letter.

"Dear Olivia,

Thank you for all your hard work over the past few months with planning our wedding, you have been extremely kind and thoughtful. It is because of this tactfulness and kindness that I am asking you a huge favour. When you read this letter we will already be on our way to our honeymoon. I know everyone will be very disappointed but I can't face the whole production that our wedding has become. Please explain to my mother, I know you will be able to find the words. It will take some time for them to forgive me but they will in time. Charles and I are having a baby and I need to take back control of my life now because I will soon have someone else to protect and be responsible for.

I hope this doesn't cause you too much trouble.

Thank you again for your help

Emily Cardew"

"Oh God!" Olivia exclaimed to the empty room. She perhaps should have seen this coming, Emily had been swept along by her parents and future in-laws, still they would all come round once they knew a baby was on the way, she thought hopefully.

Shrieks from the hallway outside her office told Olivia that Faye and Veronica had probably already discovered for themselves that Emily and Charles were missing, taking a deep breath she braced herself to go and talk to them.

Once the initial hysterics had died down and the slow and painful realisation that two hundred people would be arriving later that day to celebrate a wedding that wouldn't take place, the chaos really started. Olivia, initially the sole of discretion and tact, eventually felt the need to exert some control of the situation.

"Could we all just calm down, please. We need to decide what to do." She raised her voice above the wailing of Faye Cardew who was strangely finding more comfort from Bradley Whelps than from her own husband who was simply drinking whiskey in the bar.

Eventually it was decided that it being unlikely that they could contact many of the guests at this late time, it was better to let everyone come, have a toned down reception anyway, as all the food was prepared and everything was already paid for, and simply embrace the fact that the bride and groom, very much in love had eloped.

The day was a long and strained one for Olivia, she spent much of her time placating Faye and Veronica. Many of the guests barely noticed the fact that the actual wedding hadn't taken place, but took the opportunity to catch up with old friends, eat and drink at someone else's considerable expense and generally feel happy not to listen to boring speeches or feel obliged to eat fruit cake after a superb three course dinner. She only hoped that Emily and Charles were enjoying their brief moment of tranquillity before returning to the furore that was inevitable.

Several weeks later Olivia was racing into the bank on Flipping Bodbury high street in her lunch hour when she literally collided with Faye Cardew and Bradley Whelps coming the other way. They both called hello to her and despite her lack of time she felt obliged to stop.

"Olivia, good to see you." Bradley put out his hand and Olivia returned the friendly hand shake.

"Hello, Mr Whelps. How are Emily and Charles?" She didn't know if she was about to open a can of worms but decided it would be impossible not to enquire.

"Oh, they're fine, Emily is getting over the morning sickness now and she is so excited about the baby, mind you she's finding it hard to understand our new arrangement." Faye smiled up at Bradley and Olivia caught the look exchanged between them and noticed the way Faye squeezed his arm in an intimate gesture. Olivia not having a clue what she was talking about felt it better to flee the situation before getting further embroiled.

"Please give my best wishes to Emily and I hope all goes well with the baby." Briefly she shook hands again and disappeared into the bank.

Tracey Jones had proved such an asset to the Malmsbury Hotel that Olivia had managed to persuade Alasdair and Miranda to keep her on after the summer wedding rush had ended. One of the very positive outcomes of the Cardew wedding disaster had been the fact that Tracey had well and truly caught her future husband, hook, line and sinker in the form of Charles' best man. Mark Lester had met Charles at university, and whilst Charles had taken the acting route Mark had already established himself as an up and coming director. When the wedding reception turned into more of a wake, Tracey had taken an active role in ensuring things at least ran as smoothly as they could, given the circumstances, and this included ensnaring the best man. The joy for Tracey was that she found herself with the male equivalent of the wedding nutcase and they were currently planning their own nuptials.

When Olivia returned from lunch Tracey was busily sorting out The Flipping Bodbury annual Autumn recital and barely looked up when Olivia came in.

"You'll never guess who I just bumped into. Don't bother to guess I'll just tell you. Faye Cardew and Bradley Whelps!" Olivia looked at Tracey waiting for a reaction and was disappointed not to get even a flicker of interest.

"That's nice, how's Emily?" Tracey carried on with her work.

"Emily's fine, but you don't get it, Faye and Bradley looked together!" Olivia stressed the importance of this last bit of information.

"Yeah, well that was fairly obviously going to happen wasn't it." Still Tracey carried on with her paper shuffling.

"Somewhere you lost me on this one." Olivia responded with a sigh.

"I tried to tell you before the wedding but you were so wrapped up in all the arrangements I decided not to worry you. Faye and Bradley were snogging behind the cleaning trolley outside the bridal suite when I went to check on the room, it was really gross." An image sprang into Olivia's mind and she couldn't help agreeing with Tracey it was fairly awful.

"Poor Veronica, she must be devastated, no husband and no big wedding." Olivia felt genuinely sorry for her even though she'd driven her nuts for weeks.

"Oh, no, don't worry on that score. They swapped." Tracey looked up as if this was completely normal behaviour.

"Swapped?" Olivia was now truly lost.

"Yes, it must have started with all the wedding planning, they have swapped husbands, it all seems very amicable and it made the whole wedding disaster a lot easier to cope with, they are all getting invited to every social event going because everyone wants to have a nosy at them." Tracey seemed to accept this as quite straightforward and reasonable.

Olivia gazed out of the window absorbing this new piece of information, not only had she not realised Emily and Charles were going to do a bunk, she hadn't caught on to the wife swapping either, and come to think of it she had been the last person to hear about Tracey and the best man getting together. On reflection Olivia decided her forte was organising x-rated magic shows, drag shows and other such unromantic events and she'd leave the weddings to Tracey, as they were clearly more her forte.

The Cricket Match

The South Cotswold Cricket Club Committee convened frequently to enable the members, comprised solely of men of the area to escape their homes temporarily; avoid putting children to bed, carrying out household chores or worse still conversing with their wives. However the meeting currently underway was of the utmost importance to plan for the forthcoming match, the annual Belford Cup between the South Cotswold Cormorants and the Northampton Nailers. The rivalry between England and Australia for the Ashes paled into insignificance in comparison to that of these two teams.

Flipping Bodbury had fielded a reasonable team for the past few years and was level pegging with four wins each since the Cup had begun. Several key players had recently relocated out of the area in order to remain in work and the team's star player Dominic Hunter, a sixth-former at the nearby public school, Chartwell Hall, had broken several bones in his right hand attempting to climb back into his dormitory following an illegal night out in town. His yells of pain as the sash window smashed onto his hand had woken half of the school; thereby depriving the Cormorants of their star bowler. Dominic Hunter, hunter by name and by nature, was a blonde haired, blue eyed Adonis who would have been snapped up by the cricket association by now if it wasn't for his laziness, preference for girls and booze to training and his father's determination for him to become a lawyer in the family firm. It had caused much consternation for the rest of the cricket team when Dominic joined the previous summer because it made the rest of them look fat and old, which most of them undoubtedly were, but once he started bowling out the opposition they forgave his good looks and natural six-pack and actively sort to keep him for themselves.

"Agenda item 4, the Northants match. Anyone got news of young Dominic?" Patrick Sargeant, chairing the meeting knew this item would go on forever.

"Virtually under house arrest I believe at Chartwell, says his hand is mending but won't be fixed in time for the match. All credit to the lad though he's practicing every spare moment with his left hand." Phillip Greenaway, local estate agent and (in his own mind) lady-killer, had been keeping in touch with Dominic to assess his chances of still playing for them.

"Well let's face it, Dominic bowling left handed is still going to be better than any of us can do with our right, I say we keep him in the team." General grunts of approval met this remark; such was the desperation to win the match.

"Now, more bad news, we have been assigned Reverend Billingsgate as the Umpire for the match." Much head shaking followed this revelation as Patrick knew it would. Reverend Billingsgate, supposedly impartial in this particular match, was likely to favour the opposition. The reverend's parish of Upper Charworthy in the north of the Cotswolds had recently entered the 'Best Kept Cemetery' competition. Reverend Hopeswell of Flipping Bodbury had also entered his parish church and had won. On the morning of the judging Reverend Billingsgate had undertaken a last minute check to ensure all was immaculate and having found this to be the case retired to the rectory to work on his sermon. By the time the judges arrived they discovered vast quantities of dog pooh scattered about the place and had been most unimpressed. Reverend Billingsgate insisted it was a case of sabotage, and when Flipping Bodbury won the competition he let it be known that he believed members of the Church Committee in Flipping Bodbury to be the culprits. Needless to say nothing had been proved, but it was still a bone of contention for Reverend Billingsgate.

"There's nothing for it, we have to pull out all the stops and resort to a dirty tricks campaign if necessary." This suggestion was put forward by Ronnie Webster, new to the area, a lottery winner with a decidedly murky background, who had been allowed to join the cricket club due to the fact that he was younger than most of the others and fitter and because he splashed his money around to buy his way into acceptability.

"We don't want to venture down that route Ronnie," piped up Major Ronaldson who ran the cricket social club and was a stickler for rules and propriety.

The following Saturday afternoon the team gathered at the club for a training session. Jamie Henderson, local bar owner and seriously good looking individual was usually otherwise engaged on these occasions, but had been press-ganged into appearing for a practice at the nets by Patrick Sargeant.

"Thanks for showing up lad, we all need the practice if we're to stand a chance against Northants with Dominic injured." Patrick patted Jamie on the back and handed him a bat.

"I actually think we might need to consider some slightly less orthodox methods for next Sunday if we are going to have a prayer." Jamie moved in closer to talk to Patrick checking that no-one else was in earshot. "I say we get together a group who can be relied on for their open-mindedness about the rules and work out one or two tactics." Patrick coughed and shuffled about uncomfortably, but agreed to be at Hendersons bar that evening for a non-official club meeting.

The day of the match arrived with near perfect weather conditions, a light breeze and glorious sunshine, ensuring a good crowd to support the home team. The Cormorant's assembled in the changing rooms of the cricket pavilion lamenting the good weather, having prayed for rain all week in the hope that the match might be postponed and thus give their star bowler's injured hand time to repair. Glances were exchanged between the select few who knew that plan B was now their only hope.

The large crowd had turned out for a variety of

reasons; some to enjoy the weather, some to rally behind the Cormorants but the majority of the young, females out in force were simply there to gaze at Dominic and the Henderson brothers in their cricket whites. Major Ronaldson had persuaded the Headmaster of Chartwell Hall to release Dominic from his curfew for a few hours in order that he could play in the match, albeit left handed.

The play in the early afternoon was predictable, the strength of the visiting bowlers left the home team struggling for runs, and just as they broke for afternoon tea the home team were all out for 180. Jamie and Luke had both put up an impressive show but were outclassed by the opposition's new bowler, who Jamie felt he recognised from somewhere but couldn't quite work out where. Going in for tea he caught up with Ronnie Webster.

"We're seriously going to struggle to break their play Ronnie; we need to get things moving in our favour. Luke's going to lace the Nailers' squash with vodka, let's hope their thirsty." He made his way over to where Dominic was surrounded by groupies.

"Dominic, a word please," Jamie pulled him to one side.

"We're putting plan B into action, you know what to do?" Dominic nodded and wandered back to his admiring fans, quietly instructing the girls to do some seriously distracting sunbathing near the opposition fielders, in return for which he promised invites to the Chartwell Hall end of term ball, which guaranteed their help.

Ronnie Webster's wife adjusted her cleavage in the ladies loos, undid another button on her tight blouse and added more lip gloss. Wandering back into the bar she found her target, Reverend Billingsgate, and homed in with flattery and feigned interest in his latest parish developments. Whilst the umpire was fully engaged in conversation his eyes never leaving Chrissie's chest, Dominic had no problem pilfering the official cricket ball which the Reverend had left on the bar. Dominic hastily headed for the changing rooms where he scuffed the ball on one side to aid the spin and direction and then carefully returned it to its rightful place. Reverend Billingsgate was still busily assuring Chrissie that she would be welcomed with open arms in his parish WI.

The final assault on the opposition team came by way of Major Ronaldson's grand-daughter, Lila-belle. At 17, Lila-belle was every parent's nightmare, although her parents had little to do with her. Major Ronaldson's daughter had run off with a low ranking squaddie who had been court-martialled out of the army, she was sixteen and pregnant at the time and Major Ronaldson had disowned her. Sometime later he agreed to raise Lila-belle and provide an education for her. St Catherine's boarding school had become the lucky recipients of the child and Major Ronaldson, a widow since his wife had died in child birth took on the responsibility of Lila in the holidays. Now aged 17, with a pixie haircut, petite features and an enviable figure, she was beginning to realise her potential with the male sex. A recent school report had informed her grandfather that if Lila failed her exams, as was predicted, she would certainly have a career ahead of her as an escapologist due to the ingenious ways she found of getting out of St Catherines. Lila had had her wings clipped by the headmistress on many occasions but she was still determined to fly!

Robert Chelsey was unaccustomed to female attention. He was the youngest and best batsman on the opposition team. A serious individual, spotty, with thick rimmed glasses he was unpopular at his public school and had joined the Northants Nailers in order to please his mother who was worried about his lack of friends. Lila-belle spent the next twenty minutes feigning interest in Robert, and generally made herself so agreeable to him that by the time the teams headed back out to play his mind was very definitely not on his cricket bat.

Play resumed with the home team coming out to bowl, Dominic feeling the pressure of the task ahead and using his left arm, struggled with the first couple of overs but then gradually began to get into his stride taking out two of the Northants batsman for only 12 runs. The distraction by the girls, now stripped down to skimpy bikinis, in the line of the batsmen's vision was working a treat. When Lila-belle blew a kiss to Robert as he strode out for his innings he completely lost the plot and was bowled out for a very poor 20 runs. Despite squash and tea laced with vodka, the opponents were putting on an impressive show. When a thickly set, tall, new team member emerged from the pavilion Jamie feared the worst. The newcomer took up his position at the crease looked confident; however, something about his beard was bothering him in the heat. Jamie watched Dominic bowl to him and noticed the fluid action of his bat stroke, something just wasn't right.

Despite his best efforts Dominic was unable to out-bowl them with his left hand and the opposition retired with an impressive 230 runs victorious, but surprisingly restrained in their celebration. Jamie headed straight for the changing rooms deciding not to hang around for Belford Cup presentation, but instead he slipped out the back to the car park and to his amazement came upon one of his cricketing heroes. The new player for the Northants Nailers was also making a hasty exit, but for quite different reasons. Sir Ian Flotsam, thrice capped former England Cricket Captain, had somewhere else he needed to be that evening, having played in disguise as a favour to his uncle, the Reverend Billingsgate.

Jamie turned on his heel and headed back to the pavilion to share the glorious news and claim the match by default, feeling pious in the knowledge that his own team had mildly cheated but they had the good sense not to get caught. A victory for Flipping Bodbury after all.

En Guarde

Elizabeth Montgomery had spent a good deal of time in the summer recess organising the autumn timetable for the Flipping Bodbury WI. Alongside planning the obligatory fund raising events she was keen to add an afternoon of light exercise to aid her raging battle against her spreading waistline, this the result of too many delicious dinners with her charming companion, Major Ronaldson. Elizabeth had been toying with several ideas including the latest craze for Zumba classes, but had decided the vigorous gyrating required was not really befitting ladies of a certain age and smacked of the desperation of 'Shirley Valentine' which was not in keeping with her WI troop. Also worthy of consideration had been Wii fitness classes, until she had seen an advert on television with Dame Helen Mirren looking poised and svelte and spouting about the benefits of the product. Having been irritated by her already toned body, she felt this would demoralise rather than inspire her ladies to leap into Lycra. So she had finally settled on fencing, having attended an Open Day at Chartwell Hall boys public school, in her role as governor and had witnessed a magnificent and elegant display by Guy Picard the fencing instructor.

Guy, early thirties, blonde and lithe, captured the imagination of every woman, and a good deal of men, who had ever laid eyes on him and Elizabeth was no exception. Guy was keen to help her WI ladies with their exercise programme partly because he was constantly being nagged by Bartholomew Winters, the Headmaster of Chartwell, to forge stronger links with the community, but also because it would enable him to miss a tedious departmental meeting with the sergeant major of a PE Department Head, Angus Smythe, with whom he could never see eye to eye.

Autumn WI meetings began on a Tuesday afternoon in early September and were being held in the church hall which had recently acquired a new heating system thanks to money raised by a previous, and somewhat controversial, WI fundraising event, a dinner dance and strip-show.

"Good afternoon ladies. I hope you have all received my electronic mailing communication?" Elizabeth Montgomery paused and surveyed the gathering.

"What did she say?" whispered Maud Beachy to her neighbour on her left, Anoria Harper, the resident medium.

"She asked if you got the email," Anoria replied.

"Oh yes. Why didn't she just say that?" Maud mumbled.

"As we, the WI, embrace this technological age of electronic mailing communications, all future correspondence disseminated from Head Office will be forwarded to you ladies in this format."

"I don't see what's wrong with the post," Maud chuntered under her breath.

"I thought this autumn we would leave the jam making classes behind and undertake a little light physical activity." Elizabeth paused waiting for the groans of disapproval but surprisingly none were forthcoming. "I have enlisted the help of Guy Picard to instruct us in the art of Fencing." Again she paused, and this time there was a general muttering. "I have produced a leaflet outlining what is involved and I am hoping for a good turnout next week. Please sign your names on the list before leaving today. Shall we move onto fundraising before breaking for tea Winnie?" She looked over at her deputy who took up the next phase of the meeting.

Maud Beachy, who was operating the tea urn on a rota system, turned to Anoria who was on milk and sugar duty.

"When she said fencing in her email, I thought she meant we might be doing a gardening slot this year. I did think to myself, fencing, what about dry stone walling, well we are in the Cotswolds after all." Anoria simply nodded in response and wondered at her friend, whilst handing out the refreshments.

Further down the tea queue Chrissie Webster, one of the newest and also youngest members of the Flipping Bodbury WI, was busily informing Arlette,

"When I read fencing I said to my Ronnie, blimey Ronnie, we're only going to be learning about getting rid of stolen goods, who'd have thought it of the WI, very progressive my Ronnie thought." Poor Arlette nearly choked on her rock cake, she must remember to tell Patrick that little snippet later.

It was a motley crew that assembled for the first fencing lesson the following week. As Guy surveyed his audience he knew he had his work cut out with this group if they were even to learn the rudiments of his art. However, old Bartie Winters had been most impressed by Guy's apparently unselfish act, and brownie points with Bartie were always a good thing, especially when salary and promotion reviews were on the horizon.

"Sorry I'm late," cried Chrissie, her trainers squeaking on the wooden floor as she dashed into the church hall. "I was catching the end of Loose Women because Colin Firth was on. Sorry Elizabeth." She slid into the first available seat and smiled sweetly at Guy who was staring open-mouthed at her ensemble of shiny gold leggings and cropped vest her ample bosom spilling over the top. He quickly regained his composure and addressed the group.

"Today ladies I thought we'd begin by giving you a quick demonstration of the art of Fencing. Once you've had a chance to see the sport in action you will be able to appreciate the safety measures we must put in place, and I hope begin to understand how your general fitness levels can be greatly improved by training for this sport."

Guy already dressed in his full combat regalia dropped his mask into place and assumed the starting position with a flourish of his foil. His opponent, Marcus Derby, was only too happy to be helping out today with his favourite master, as he was also missing double French.

A flamboyant display then took place during which there was much 'umming' and 'aahing' by the ladies as they absorbed the scene before them. Chrissie, desperate to make a good impression on her fellow WI ladies as a new recruit, was avidly committing every move to memory.

"I could watch fit young men do this all day," Winnie giggled to Arlette who was sitting to her right.

"I'm getting a bit of a sweat on and we haven't even started yet," Arlette replied.

"Shush." Elizabeth Montgomery hissed at them like a headmistress chastising naughty schoolgirls, but this only made them giggle more.

With the stamping and thrusting of the action in front of them, the ladies were transfixed, if a little daunted by the prospect of actually having to attempt it themselves. Guy and Marcus made the lunges, twists and turns look effortless, and the clashing of steel upon steel resounded around the hall. With the culmination of the fight came a spontaneous round of applause as the dashing heroes removed their masks.

"So now ladies, we begin," Guy informed his audience. "Marcus will hand you a foam foil and we will start by learning some safety precautions and rudimentary positions."

Drew and Blair Bantham, unofficial members of the WI, but easily the most hardworking when it came to fundraising and ideas, leapt to their feet.

"I can't remember the last time I held anything so

floppy!" Blair shrieked to Winnie as he wielded the sponge foil. Arlette already having difficulty with keeping a straight face collapsed in a heap, relieved to have taken Winnie's advice about the extra Tena Lady, her bladder control not being what it used to be; especially when she laughed.

"Blair dear, if you are going to keep up with the nasty innuendoes I will have to ask you to leave." Elizabeth, the model of correctness, chastised him.

"Sorry Lizbeth darling, I'll try and keep him in line," replied Drew, who shot a scolding look at Blair.

"I hope he won't poke me with his sharp sabre," Blair retorted to Winnie under his breath, reducing her to hysterics once again and sending her scurrying to the loos.

The afternoon continued in much the same vein, and Guy began to wonder if he should have simply put up with staff meetings instead as this was proving to be hard work. However, the ladies were undeniably having a fine time and everyone left the hall later, tired but having thoroughly enjoyed themselves.

The bar in Hendersons was packed as usual on a busy Thursday evening. At a large table in the far corner the Chartwell Hall sports department were holding a meeting to discuss extra-curricular activities. Guy had momentarily escaped the waffle by going to the bar and was just being served when he was joined by Angus Smythe.

"Can I get you one?" he asked reluctantly.

"Bottle of Bud please, Guy." Angus waved his empty bottle at the barmaid and she passed him another cold beer.

"Cheers," Guy offered.

"How's the fencing going with the old biddies?" Angus enquired, his tone clearly disparaging.

"They're coming on really well actually." This was a huge exaggeration on Guy's part. Three weeks into the lessons, none of his ladies really had a clue, although a couple of them were particularly keen if not actually skilled, but there was no way he was going to let Angus know that.

"I thought a little wager would give you something to work towards." Angus took a large swig of his beer. "£500 says you can't get a team together to enter the Cheltenham Salver." He waited for Guy's reaction.

"I can get a team together for that." Guy responded positively outwardly, whilst inwardly his brain was whirling away negatively.

"The team needs to be placed in the medals, minimum bronze," Angus smirked. Guy, if he didn't need his job so badly, would have loved to knock his teeth out. He shouldn't accept the wager but Angus knew he wouldn't refuse the challenge.

"The Salver is in six weeks, that's no time at all to bring on complete novices," he stated.

"Think of it as career development." Patting him patronisingly on the back, Angus put down another empty bottle and left the bar.

By the fourth week of fencing lessons Guy decided to risk using steel foils which produced a great deal of chatter and excitement.

"Ladies, I have brought with me chest protectors and visors which are essential items of safety equipment. When we become more experienced we will add the entire uniform but for now this will do." As Guy began to hand out the plastic body armour the group deteriorated into chaos as much hilarity ensued from their trying to squeeze themselves into these garments.

"I do think Guy," began Winnie, "that your average fencing lady must be a little bit flat-chested." She was struggling to squash her ample endowments into place but the side Velcro straps were straining to their utmost.

Chrissie was making a great show of squeezing her delightful assets into the plastic contraption, and was receiving one to one assistance from Marcus, who was only too happy to help.

"Well we should have more success with the face masks," remarked Guy, wondering if the lesson would ever get underway.

"Do me up Drewy," called Blair to his partner in crime, "I'm not used to being so restricted." Drew, having warned Blair to behave this week or they would be thrown out, yanked on the Velcro straps and nearly winded Blair, who retorted,

"So Guy do I get a cod-piece?" There followed five minutes of madness while Drew and Blair fastened their manhood protectors, and everyone except Guy was utterly helpless with laughter.

"So sexy the clash of metal on metal," Blair announced to Chrissie Webster as he waved his foil majestically in the air.

"Please remember everyone that these are serious pieces of kit." Guy despaired of Blair, who failed to take anything seriously.

"As usual we will begin with a warm-up and then practice our lunges and positions. En garde!" As Guy wandered around the room calling out instructions and correcting arm and leg positions he was also looking out for any potential team members for the Cheltenham Salver, but judging by current standards it would be a complete disaster. Today Guy had also enlisted the help of several of the sixth formers from Chartwell who were all skilful fencers hoping that this would inspire his aged apprentices.

"Aren't they lithe?" Chrissie remarked to Joan Sidewell, her fencing partner. "Lovely fit young bodies," she drooled.

Joan Sidewell, who in her younger days had been something of a looker herself, was far too intent on perfecting her parries and counter parries to be bothered about young men. Guy kept informing her that her wrist needed to be more flexible, but having suffered repetitive strain injury from years of typing she was struggling to perfect the fluid action required.

"Elizabeth your tip is pointing to the ceiling again, you must aim it at Maud, she is the enemy after-all." In order to explain this more fully, Guy lunged at Maud who shrieked and jumped backwards through sheer terror. "A very good example of a counter reverse move, Maud, well done," Guy exclaimed to a thoroughly terrified Maud Beachy whilst moving onto his next pairing.

Drew Bantham was showing much better progress now that Guy had swapped his partner to Anoria Harper.

"Bend the knee as far as you can Drew," Guy was telling him, "the greater the length of the lunge the greater the thrust. If you watch clips of the Olympic team on YouTube you'll see they practically get their knee to the floor in a lunge." He demonstrated and Drew tried to copy him but a terrible sound of material ripping accompanied his attempt as his trousers split down the back and he and Anoria collapsed in hysterics. Guy retreated to the side of the hall and watched as the group went through their patterns mentally assessing their potential. Chrissie Webster was now being shown a lunge by Tom Masters, a superb fencer at just 17 years of age, and clearly under his instruction she was allowing herself to relax into the moves, and actually made some very reasonable attempts.

Elizabeth Montgomery had all the finesse of a carthorse lumbering down the piste, waving her foil as if fending off a mugger she stamped and bellowed ungraciously. Whereas Molly and Dolly Masters, who were svelte and nimble, showed signs of some reasonable wrist action.

"This is playing havoc with my sciatic nerve, Dolly dear." Elizabeth was complaining to Dolly as she thumped towards her brandishing her foil. Dolly simply counter parried and gracefully lunged towards her with her blade held high, the hilt in line with her face and once again scored a direct hit, much to

Elizabeth's chagrin but the performance did not go unnoticed by Marcus.

At the end of a frustrating hour Marcus and Guy were packing away the equipment.

"It's hopeless isn't it?" Guy remarked.

"There are some potential fencers," Marcus replied trying to sound encouraging.

"Let me buy you something to eat at Hendersons and see if we can work out a list of possible competitors." Guy's offer was eagerly accepted as Marcus was happy to miss shepherd's pie in the refectory at Chartwell.

Sitting in front of an open fire half an hour later, Guy's mood had barely improved.

"We are going to need a team of four and a reasonable substitute just in case. I'm struggling to get the four let alone adding a sub." Guy moaned.

"Let's go through who we've got." Marcus suggested; a scrap of paper and pen in hand. "Chrissie has natural rhythm and fluidity, once she's stopped shaking her boobs and being ditsy. She's got a good lunge and a flexible wrist." Marcus blushed slightly as Jamie Henderson, owner of the wine bar, approached their table just as Marcus was speaking.

"Now Marcus, that's no way to talk about a married lady!" Jamie laughed. "Heard about your little wager Guy. How's it going?"

"No-one's supposed to know about it," Guy answered looking around furtively, "especially not the WI, I'll never get them to agree to a competition."

Jamie laughed and produced a little black notebook from his back pocket.

"Oh God," muttered Guy, "you're running a book on this aren't you?"

"No pressure Guy, but the odds against you at the moment, I'm taking 8-1 that you can't get your team placed in the medals." Jamie smiled at his friend. "Still, I've got faith in you matey, I know you can do it," he continued insincerely.

"You haven't seen them Jamie, there's only three weeks left, I haven't got a prayer. We're trying to sort out a team but it's useless," Guy responded.

"Actually I think the Masters sisters have got potential." Marcus interrupted going back to his list, "if you give them some encouragement they bloom, they're strong and they listen to every instruction. Put Drew in and drop Blair and you will see he's not bad either. The only other hopeful I think is Anoria."

Jamie began chuckling at this point, having had an interesting séance with Anoria in the past he couldn't see her as a swords person, but what did he know?

"I'll leave you to it lads. It'll all be worth it if you manage to wipe the smile off that smug bugger's face – Angus needs knocking down a peg or two." Jamie returned to the bar leaving Guy and Marcus to review their team.

"That's it then. Chrissie Webster, Molly and Dolly Masters, and Drew Bantham; with Anoria Harper as sub." Guy picked up his drink and downed the remainder. "I think I need another one."

Alicia Hunter, part-time barmaid at Hendersons Wine Bar, was as good at eavesdropping as she was at pulling pints. Having overheard the wager between the gorgeous Guy and smarmy old Angus, she had decided to try and up Guy's chances of winning by immediately texting her younger brother Dominic, one of Guy's star pupils. All the students at Chartwell hated angry Angus, as he was known, and Dominic had instantly text back saying he was definitely up for a challenge. Alicia, made sure she caught up with Winnie Waterman during her regular pre-meeting lunch with Arlette the next day.

"Dominic is willing to give extra coaching to the team members that Guy has selected, but Guy mustn't know about it – we may need to gen up on a few cheating techniques if we're going to stand a chance – don't worry ladies – we can rely on Dominic for that," Alicia was informing Winnie and Arlette.

"Poor Guy, he's worked so hard teaching us these past few weeks, why has Angus got it in for him?" Winnie asked, always one to champion the underdog.

"Well, Guy's younger, fitter and well in with Bartie, rumour has it Bartie may be fast tracking him to deputy head and he's not even run his own department yet. Angus is a bully, real old school, no-one likes him at Chartwell, and he just wants Guy to fail." Alicia was always in the know on local gossip; she also had a thumping crush on Guy and was keen to help him out.

"We will need to get the team together every evening for the next three weeks or we haven't got a prayer of getting placed in the medals," she continued, "even if we do play dirty."

"I'm not sure we can condone cheating," Arlette began uncertainly.

"Don't be ridiculous Lette, we will use every trick in the book if it means helping Guy to win his wager – the WI won't let him down. We've an empty barn up at our place, it's got lighting but it'll be cold; still it's out of town so there's less chance of anyone being spotted." Winnie downed the last of her wine and gathered her belongings together. "Come on Lette we need to go and rally the troops." With that the pair headed off towards the Church hall conspiring as they went.

The 'illegal' training sessions took place in the barn at Winnie's farm at 7pm each evening and Dominic, who had been shocked by his potential sportspeople at his first encounter, was nonetheless impressed by their sheer determination and willingness to put in the work needed. A natural sportsman, he was also fiercely driven to succeed at anything he attempted and this particular challenge was to be no exception. The Cheltenham Salver, or Beginners Cup as it was known, was merely a county trophy but to Dominic the importance of his team being successful was immense. He enlisted the help of several of his fencing classmates, and being the wide boy he was instructed them to teach the WI team members not only the legitimate moves but one or two less orthodox tactics to help them out should they need it. This should stand them in good stead against some of the other beginners. Above all the group wanted to succeed for Guy's sake and this made even Dolly Masters, the most timid of the Masters sisters, willing to consider bending the rules if need be. The hardest part of the secret training sessions was the problem of the boys escaping from Chartwell each evening. Dominic was well used to climbing out of his dormitory window on his own and using the ivy that grew in abundance to aid his return, but getting four of them out each evening was proving hazardous with the old plant pulling away from its grip on the bricks, until it was inevitable that a fall would occur. Tom Masters had to attempt to peddle to Winnie's with a sprained ankle and despite it being bandaged and wrested whilst he watched the training session it suffered a further setback when he attempted to gain re-entry via the ivy climbing ladder to his room at Chartwell. No-one complained however, it just added to their determination.

Preparations for the big day were well underway albeit surreptitiously. Everyone knew that the trip to Cheltenham was not just a day out for the WI fencing ladies (including honorary girlie members Drew and Blair) but the pressure of pretending not to know about the competition was proving to be too much for some, and there was much twittering and whispering going on. Guy was becoming more on edge by the day. Using the premise that his team had merely been selected to perform a short demonstration at the competition in order to showcase the sport for the older person, Guy had been able to organise complete regalia required for competing. The only reason for not telling his team his true intention of entering them into the competition, was because he feared a rebellion would take place and they would refuse to take part, little did he appreciate the gusto of the Flipping Bodbury WI when their pecker was raised.

The car park of Hendersons Wine Bar was a hive of activity with the WI arriving to catch the coach to

Cheltenham, bustling around in high spirits, anticipation and nerves showing among those who were heading off to compete. After much herding his flock Guy did one last head count and told the driver to set off. He hoped the chatter and banality would diminish on the way.

Looking out of the window, Guy was trying and failing to decide the best course of action. If he came clean about the competition, would they decide to pull out? There again if he didn't tell them it might become a fiasco, especially if Drew was his usual flippant self. £500.00 was a lot to lose, not to mention the real reason for Angus's wager, which above all was to humiliate and ridicule Guy publicly.

"Milky coffee, anyone?" Winnie unearthed an array of odd plastic flask lids from her bag.

"Count me in." Blair raised his hand, knowing full well that a generous hint of 'The Famous Grouse', always accompanied Winnie's offerings of coffee!

"Let's have a sing-song," called Drew, handing out photocopied song sheets, along with the box of homemade flapjacks. Half an hour later the WI members were in full voice when Guy stood up, unable to contain himself any longer.

"Can we please have some quiet? None of you seem to be taking this seriously," he shouted.

Chrissie piped up,

"It's only a demonstration Guy, stop getting your knickers in a twist." She knew full well why he was so snappy and hoped this would prompt him to come clean, after all they all knew what was really going on.

"I'm sorry. I didn't sleep much last night. It must be catching up with me." His voice trailed off and he blushed as the whole coach stared at him. The rest of the journey passed without the jollity of the first half, and finally Guy, after much persuasion from Marcus, decided that forewarned was forearmed (which seemed highly appropriate under the circumstances) and decided to come clean as soon as they got off the coach.

Winnie was clucking around the group in her mother hen role and whispering advice when Guy approached them,

"Well now ladies, and gentleman," he nodded to Drew, "I feel I should apologise in advance for a slight untruth I have told. I have got you here under false pretences today." He glanced at the team members to gauge their reactions as he continued. "It isn't a demonstration that you are here for, but the Beginners Cup – now before you all panic, I wouldn't have put you in for it if I didn't think you could make the grade." He paused to await a torrent of abuse he felt was inevitable.

"Rubbish," declared Drew winking at the others, "you entered us to win a wager against angry Angus and you don't think we stick a chance." Drew spoke for everyone as he said this and Guy had the good grace to look suitably uncomfortable.

"Hell's bells," was all he could say.

"Now, young Guy," began Elizabeth, "we WI know how to rise to a challenge, this team is going to give it a go and that's as much as anyone can ask of them." Elizabeth beamed at the assembled group with pride.

"How long have you known about this?" Guy asked, amazed and inspired by their determination.

"Three weeks, and Dominic's been doing a great job of extra coaching. You've got a lot of support locally Guy, we'll do our best," Drew tried to reassure him.

After a quick pep talk and much shaking of hands Guy rushed off to register his team. Allowing himself to feel mildly encouraged when he discovered the referee for the event was Desmond Filcher, Guy momentarily began to relax. Desmond was well known on the fencing circuit for being both an incredibly impressive swordsman when he was in his prime but also now he was more famous for his impressive drinking ability. This had the natural effect of making him somewhat lax about his judgement after a heavy session the night before, and Guy could tell that based on the Alka-Seltzers he was downing the pubs of Cheltenham had undoubtedly received his patronage the previous evening. Guy had spent much of the last of his afternoon lessons with his protégés going through the rules of competition, and had despatched them with a set of DVDs to watch in order to observe the finer points of the game in the hope that some inspiring play might ensue.

When he returned Marcus was giving the team some final instructions.

"Molly, you're up first. No need to panic; let me just run through the format. You begin on the on guard line, foil held upwards at chin height, just like we do in class, but don't forget to salute to your opponent and the ref before you begin otherwise you'll forfeit the match, likewise bow at the end. Just remember whoever reaches 15 points first is the winner but if the nine minutes elapse before reaching maximum points whoever has the most will win." Marcus could see that this was beginning to worry Molly and hastily added, "just do what you have been doing in Dominic's lessons and keep cool, the fencer that gets uptight is the one who makes silly mistakes."

"I wish I wasn't first," answered Molly

"Nonsense dear, get it over and done with," interrupted Winnie, who was still fussing round everyone.

Some ten minutes later, having rushed to the loo several times, Molly took up her position on the piste. She raised her foil, saluted the ref and her opponent a tall, lean young man, and assumed the on guard position, her knees knocking and her hand shaking. The referee called 'play', and Molly lunged into action. Seven minutes of fencing following with some adept moves from Molly but she did not manage to out play her opponent, and he reached the illusive fifteen points before her. Much hand shaking and back-patting took place when she re-joined her team, but her disappointment was clear for all to see. Guy warmly welcomed her back to the competitors' bench. Dolly, who was up next, then managed a victory over an energetic but clumsy teenage girl who stomped off the piste in a fury at being beaten by someone of advanced years.

"I'm so glad that's over," Molly whispered to

Dolly, "I hope we don't go through to the play-offs, I don't want to do it again!"

With his best player up next Guy hardly dared to get his hopes up as Drew grabbed his mask and foil. Despite his camp behaviour most of the time, Guy had witnessed some promising moves from Drew in class and believed if he wasn't being distracted by Blair he could actually do well.

"Good luck my darling, just think of Zorro!" Blair called out to him, much to the hilarity of the neighbouring teenage competitors.

Drew turned back to his team mates and Elizabeth, never normally known to use modern gestures, strode towards him for a high five. As their hands slapped together in mid-air a resounding crack could be heard and Drew let out a blood curdling yell.

"Oh my goodness, Drew. Are you alright?" gasped Elizabeth.

"Bloody hell, I think you've broken my wrist, it hurts like hell." Drew clutching his wrist was doubled over in pain. The rest of the WI group were gasping and clamouring round to help as the St John's Ambulance lady, who had looked bored sat at the edge of the competition area all afternoon, now rushed forward clutching her first aid bag and Drew, with Blair flapping behind, was whisked off out of the arena.

"What now then?" asked Elizabeth, her normal brisk manner returning, all concern for Drew having evaporated. "Guy, what are we going to do if Drew can't fence? The referee is waiting."

"Put Chrissie up next and then we'll need to use

our sub." Guy looked at Anoria whose normally ruddy complexion was now ashen.

Chrissie grabbed her mask and headed up onto the competing area to a round of applause from the rest of the competitors who had all witnessed the debacle.

"Hold your nerve Chrissie, love, just pretend you're back in Winnie's barn with Dominic," Molly suggested.

"Actually Molly that's not the most helpful image right now," muttered Chrissie who had a huge crush on young Dominic; even if she was cradle snatching.

Head held high Chrissie strode onto the piste. With her normally blonde curls recently dyed to an amazing raven, her breaches clinging to her thighs and her push-up bra further enhancing her assets, she looked every bit the saucy madam. Saluting and raising her foil to begin, she mentally went completely into the zone in order to do her bit for the WI who she so wanted to impress.

"It'd take a monk not to be put off his stroke by Chrissie's movements," Marcus whispered to Guy who was staring fixedly at the match in front of him.

"I'll accept a win on any terms today. Let's face it she's got it so she may as well flaunt it," Guy replied.

A matter of minutes later Chrissie returned triumphant to the team bench, having displayed a truly impressive performance against a middle aged man who had been somewhat distracted by her exaggeratedly sensual swordplay opposite him.

Guy was allowing himself to feel proud of his team

but reality dawned again and his greatest challenge was to persuade Anoria, the sub, to step into the breach.

"If you don't play Anoria," Guy was saying to a visibly shaking Anoria, "we will have to forfeit the match. Make your decision Anoria, can I go and declare a sub to the ref or are we going home defeated?" Guy knew this was unfair because Anoria was truly scared but he had no other choice but to try and force her into it.

"I can't let the team down," she spluttered, "I'll give it a go."

"Take a slug of coffee, Anoria; it'll calm your nerves." Winnie offered helpfully, but Guy grabbed the flask off her knowing full well that it was heavily laced with whiskey, and not wanting Anoria drunk as well as scared to death he refused to give it back until after the match.

With her knees knocking together and her hands shaking, Anoria made tentative steps towards the piste. The WI team mates encouraged her on but her heart was pounding so loud in her ears she couldn't hear anything they said to her. 'Remember to salute," she kept saying to herself. Reaching the referees desk she saluted and turned to take her position on the on guard line and for the first time had to look directly at her opponent. There before her stood a sturdy looking young man, probably late teens, he was slashing his foil through the air to warm up and turned to his supporters and laughed mockingly at Anoria. Guy, watching from the side-lines, felt sick to the stomach and knew what this was costing Anoria in nerves to be able to remain standing there. Both fencers bowed to each other and Desmond Filcher called 'play'. The young opponent leapt into action taking Anoria by surprise and she was instantly hit, the electronic bleeper sounded and she jumped out of her skin. There followed several minutes of humiliation for Anoria who went to pieces with every further hit but in all credit to her undying wish to support her team she carried on. Such was the growing confidence of the young opponent that he started to show off and exaggerate his successes to the audience. The WI team members and supporters began to boo him, but this did nothing to help Anoria until the final bell went and he threw his foil into the air in celebration, running from the piste to his team members, a shriek went out from the piste.

"Stop!" yelled Anoria. "He didn't salute, he's forfeited the match!" A cheer went up from the WI team and supporters, and Desmond Filcher, who was a stickler for the rules and hated cocky players, immediately called him back and announced Anoria as the winner.

The WI team ran onto the piste and hugged the life out of Anoria, who would have loved to have won the match by her fencing skills but was happy to accept a win on any terms.

"Bloody hell," said Arlette who was watching Guy's reaction, "That means we're through to the play-offs."

Guy was emotionally exhausted but absolutely thrilled for his team, himself, but mostly for Anoria who had tried so hard. Now he had to choose who to put forward for the singles play off. Four teams had qualified for the second round and they would need to play each other. This round required fifteen minutes of play between two fencers and the number of hits each player managed in that time would be placed on the leader board to determine gold, silver and bronze places, there being no prize for coming fourth.

With a break for lunch Guy had only an hour to decide who to put forward for the play-offs, leaving the chaos of the WI camp behind he and Marcus went outside to work out a strategy. Blair had been texting Arlette from the hospital to let them know that Drew's wrist had been plastered, and they hoped to be back in time for the final showdown, despite the pain Drew didn't want to miss watching the play-offs. Winnie was busy texting Dominic for advice on how to handle the play-offs, he immediately answered with a couple of underhand suggestions which Winnie deleted as soon as she'd read them.

"It's got to be Chrissie," Guy was saying to Marcus out in the foyer. "She's the only one who looked commanding out there."

"I think Dolly could do it," replied Marcus, "she won her round convincingly and she's calm under pressure."

"Let's face it we've won two games largely by default, I know Dolly won her game on merit but I think Chrissie's got the balls to carry us through. This is terrible, I'd just presumed if we got this far I'd be putting Drew in, silly idiot wrecked everything by breaking his wrist."

"I don't think he's too happy about it either,"

snapped Blair, walking into the foyer just as Guy was speaking.

"I'm sorry Blair, of course he didn't mate, I'm just struggling to know what to do," Guy replied.

"Simple, put Chrissie in and get her to strut her stuff. She'll walk it." Blair flounced off with a pale looking Drew to find the others.

The tannoy announcement came through a few minutes later to request all teams to enter the name of their competing fencer for the play-offs.

"This is it then folks," Guy spoke to his team, "Chrissie, we're all behind you, just do your best." Guy led her forward to the referees table to register. As the other competitors gave their names Chrissie couldn't help but feel completely outclassed, she had been watching attentively throughout the other matches and knew that most of these other players had much more experience than she had. Over the past months Chrissie had worked hard to be accepted into the WI; as a lottery winner and former beauty salon owner she was very different to the rest of the more traditional members of the Flipping Bodbury WI, she was also a fair bit younger but they had actually accepted Chrissie with her friendly nature and naïve ways immediately, if only she would realise that she had nothing to prove to them.

Once standing in position on the piste she felt nerves wash over her and then a smug, leering smirk from her opponent put her firmly back into the right mind set and she resolved to do her best. Saluting over, and masks dropped into place, the fifteen minutes began. At first her game was guarded and her opponent, a slightly portly, spotty faced youth who Chrissie imagined spent most of his time alone, probably with men's magazines shoved under his bed, took the first few hits and Chrissie was concentrating so hard on her defence she was unable to get a strike. But just when she needed it most, her inner strength revived. She knew many in Flipping Bodbury referred to her and hubby Ronnie as 'chavs made good' but here she was representing her WI and playing the sport of kings. With a sweep of inspiration she redoubled her efforts. Leering Larry opposite her now represented every single person who had ever put her down in the past and with a new found confidence she began to wipe the floor with him. Hit after hit set off the bleeper until the sweat was running into her eyes and she felt she would buckle under. Finally the bell rang for end of play and she had scored 17 hits to Larry's 8. This time the victory was sweeter because she had won it on merit not on sexual prowess. Remembering Guy's mantra about saluting she made a considerable show of acknowledging her opponent and the ref before turning to face the admiration of her team mates. All they had to do now was to hope she had scored enough hits to be placed in the medals. Leering Larry, who had no respect for women, especially ones approaching middle age and opposing him in his sport, threw down his mask and stormed off the piste.

"Fantastic Chrissie," called Guy as she was lifted off her feet by Blair and surrounded by the others. "You were incredible," he told her.

They quickly settled down to watch the remaining qualifiers go through their matches; everyone was on tenterhooks, with much wringing of hands and biting of nails. Chrissie most of all was desperate to have done enough to get them placed; she was promising God to be a better person if only she could achieve this for her team.

After what seemed like an eternity, Desmond Filcher picked up the mike to make the announcements for the medal board.

"In third place, bronze medal goes to The Westonbirt Youth Centre." Much calling and clapping accompanied this announcement, and the fencer for Westonbirt went up to receive his medal and team trophy. Guy's heart sank believing they were doomed to fourth place and thus no medal.

"In second place, silver medal goes to The Flipping Bodbury WI." The cheer that went up from the WI supporters nearly lifted the roof off the sports hall. Guy leapt into the air and grabbed hold of Chrissie, everyone was shrieking with joy. Somehow moments later Chrissie freed herself in order to go and receive her medal and the team silver trophy. She was ecstatic, as were the rest of the group and nobody paid any attention to the announcement for gold medal, that not being important to them at all. Securing Guy's medal placing was all that mattered and they had done that with knobs on.

Winnie immediately text Dominic, "Champagne is on me, we got silver, tell Angus to stick that in his pipe and smoke it!" She then text Jamie Henderson to tell him he was going to be paying out a fortune in betting winnings and to hang the flags out for the conquering heroes returning home.

"I say Guy, I think with a bit more practice we could take on the Regional Championships next. I shall write up a piece to go into the WI newsletter as soon as we get back," remarked Elizabeth as they gathered their belongings to leave.

"I think, Elizabeth, at this rate we could be heading for London 2012," Guy replied jokingly, although by the look on Elizabeth's face she had clearly taken him seriously.

The coach trip back to Flipping Bodbury was an even livelier affair than on the way there, and this time Guy was singing the loudest, aided by several celebratory swigs of Winnie's whiskey warmer!

The Introduction!

Bridget Waterman sat on a tall bar stool in Hendersons Wine Bar watching as Luke mixed her a cocktail and languished in the warm setting; a far cry from the cold outside.

"So what's in this one?" She asked.

"It's two shots of vodka, one shot of crème de cassis, topped up with pineapple juice and lots of ice. I call it 'The Introduction'." Adding a very long straw, he handed it to her.

"Not bad. Not bad at all." She replied, taking a sip. "Very easy to knock back; a few of these and you wouldn't care who you accepted a date from!" She continued with a slurp.

"Why is January such a flat month? Christmas is over and there's nothing to look forward to, unless of course, you can go skiing or you're dating someone who could afford to treat you," chipped in Alicia; Hendersons trusty barmaid. She was busily stacking wine glasses still warm from the dishwasher, more than a little preoccupied with the January blues.

"It's also one of our quietest months too," remarked Jamie as he wandered in with two crates of Euro-fizz and joined in with the moaning. "I've been wondering how we can boost business. How about a themed happy hour? Perhaps a wine promotion?"

"No, everyone does that." Luke dismissed this idea just as the main door opened and a blast of cold, wintry air announced the arrival of more customers.

"Hello everyone! What do we all know?" Drew and Blair Bantham wandered in wearing matching snoods and knitted skull caps. Luke immediately began to snigger.

"These were Christmas presents thank you very much Luke, and you can take that smirk off your beautiful face, we can so carry this look off!"

"Two G&Ts is it?" Luke enquired smiling.

"Make that three," called Phillip Greenaway. He paused in the doorway slowly unravelling a long, cashmere scarf. "It looks suspiciously like snow to me, but then it is January what can you expect?"

"We were just saying how boring this time of year is after the excitement of Christmas," Alicia said bringing Phillip up to date with the general conversation.

From the other end of the bar Bridget began to sing tunelessly.

"Oh Holy Night."

"'We'll have whatever she's having. Hold the G&T Luke. What is Bridget drinking anyway?" asked Drew.

"It's my cocktail of the month. I'm calling it 'The Introduction'." He answered passing the cocktail list to Drew.

"We could offer a free bottle of house wine with every table of four booked? Or what about unlimited soft drinks for the designated driver, that has to be a draw?" Jamie suggested, having wandered in from the kitchen with replenished bowls of bar snacks.

"Perfect: Alcohol, nibbles and beautiful women! What more could you ask for after a long day in the office?" Phillip remarked as he removed further layers of winter clothing and hung his coat up on the rack.

"Well actually a busy bar would be good!" Replied Jamie half-heartedly.

"Business not too good?" Phillip asked

"Bit down on last year. We were just discussing ways to boost our January sales, something that will bring in new trade as well as our regulars; get people mixing that sort of thing."

"That's it!" said Drew excitedly. "A speed dating evening would bring in a lot of business it's all the rage. Ticket-only entry would mean you could control how many attend. It would be a riot. You could promote your cocktail at the same time. Let's face it; this town is teaming with singletons, what better way to get people together." Drew was never one to be deterred when he had an idea.

"I'll help you organise it Drew," Bridget called from the end of the bar. "We could do with something to spice up the ailing love-lives around here. It's fine being young free and single but only if you're having some fun with it. Another drink please bartender, this is delicious!"

"Now you see Bridget, I believe in magnamy myself. None of this sowing wild oats for me." Blair gazed at Drew as he spoke.

"I think you mean, monogamy, dearest," Drew replied laughing.

"Oh well whatever, I'm a one guy kind of guy. Well, actually come to mention it, if young Guy Picard was to poke his Foil in my direction I might be tempted to make an exception." He nodded knowingly at the assembled group.

"I reckon Guy could even turn a straight bloke gay," Jamie remarked. His friend Guy Picard, Fencing instructor at Chartwell Boys school was a lethal combination: athletic, attractive and intelligent. "We'd sell a lot of tickets if we could get him to come to the speed dating."

"Somehow I doubt he'd agree," Bridget responded wistfully.

"Well then, it looks like we're having a speed dating evening; a Friday night would be good, let's go for the 24th that gives us enough time to get the posters printed," Luke called across to Jamie, "It's never too soon to advertise, so write that up on the board behind the bar, ticket-only, to start at 7.30pm sharp. Pour some of those cocktails Luke, we better ensure they're up to standard!"

Crossing the road and heading for the Post Office, Miranda Crossley clutched her packages and put her collar up against the wind. She stifled a moan as she entered and was immediately wedged in the doorway because the queue was so long; the returning of unwanted Christmas items caused even more problem than when they were first posted out.

"Morning Miranda, hope we'll be seeing you on the 24th at Hendersons?" Drew shook the rain from his umbrella and tucked into the end of the queue behind her.

"For what?" she asked timidly.

"The Speed Dating evening. Very popular in America you know. Tickets are £10.00 which includes a drink and remember you only get five minutes with each so if he's not your type you simply move on to the next, no being stuck for hours on a first date that's going nowhere." Drew's sales pitch was flowing.

"'I don't think that's my sort of thing," she replied awkwardly. "I wouldn't know what to say for a start."

"Not a problem, after one of Luke & Jamie's cocktails your inhibitions will be out the window." Miranda still looked reluctant and there followed a further ten minutes of discussion about who would be there and what to expect, her being a captive audience for Drew whilst queuing.

"I'll tell them to put you down for one, ooh looks like your turn next. More details to follow as they say. If you need help selecting just the right outfit Blair and I will be only too happy to help. That Jason Gardiner is an inspiration." Drew prodded her forward to the now vacant cashier as Miranda was still mumbling excuses which fell on deaf ears. Drew however, felt pleased with himself as another dater was mentally added to his list. He was anxious to call on all the eligible females he knew to help make the evening a success in a way only one half of a smug couple could do, and he was always keen to find ways to liven up a winter's eve especially when a little match-making was on the cards.

"Olivia, Olivia," called Bridget as she nipped out of the bank, having spied her friend crossing the road. "Fancy a coffee? I wanted to tell you about the speed dating evening at Hendersons. Do you fancy going?" Bridget Waterman, youngest daughter of Winnie and Cedric Waterman, was visiting home for a few days from her apprenticeship in London where she was studying to become a theatrical director. Her appreciation for the Henderson boys never failed to entice her to volunteer for worthy events.

"Oh well, I'm not sure," Olivia began reluctantly. "I might be working," she added noncommittally as she was firmly directed into "A Bit of what you Fancy" tea shop on the corner of the high street. They were immediately thrown into a world of doilies and lace, and the smell of homemade baking and freshly ground coffee filled the air.

"I'm going. It should be a hoot, come on live a little," Bridget teasingly mocked her friend. Olivia Beckwith worked for Crossley hotels, running the events side of the Malmsbury Spa Hotel which, under her guidance and expertise, had become an established wedding venue. Olivia had been at school with Bridget's sister, Jessica, and the girls had all remained firm friends.

Clemmy Hunter, owner of A Bit of What you Fancy, was busy replacing an empty cake stand with a new display of sumptuous cupcakes.

"Hello Bridget, love, what can I get for you?" Clemmy brushed her hands on her apron and placed a fresh tray on the counter. "Oh, by the way, tell your mum I'll pick her up on Thursday about 7pm."

"Two filter coffees with warm milk please. Where are you and mum off to then?" Bridget asked, placing two of the cupcakes onto the tray in the hope that a delicious offering might sway Olivia.

"We're going to Drew and Blair's. Their having a Pampered Chef night, apparently there's a demonstration on producing the perfect cupcake." Clemmy sounded a touch snooty.

"That'll be a bit like taking coals to Newcastle for you Clemmy," she replied, trying not to laugh and having paid for the coffees and cakes she returned to the matter in hand.

"Oh, look there's a table free by the window." She projected Olivia in that direction and turned her attention back to their earlier conversation. "The speed dating's just a bit of fun, and you never know you might meet someone nice. We can go together, safety in numbers and all that."

"I'm really not sure, Bridget, I've not dated for some time." Olivia settled herself at the table and steeled herself for a lecture.

"I won't take no for an answer, so you'll need to get your slap on and be there at 7.00pm. I'm getting you a ticket anyway so you have no choice. Anyway, Miranda's going so we'll all be able to compare notes afterwards." Olivia sipped her coffee as she allowed Bridget to bluster on knowing that further protest was useless.

With only a few days left before the big night Drew was once again in the bar giving Jamie an update on progress.

"I've managed to sell thirty tickets Jamie, so that's potentially fifteen couples but if we could get a couple more men that would be good because there's no shortage of women. I'll leave it to you to speak to Tristram and Kieran, it will do them good to have an evening with the opposite sex. Being in their professions, it's no wonder they're both still single! It's hard for a woman to fancy a man who spends his days with his hand up a cow's bottom." Drew was standing at the bar with a notebook in his hand ticking off the points on his list whilst Jamie stocked up on mixers. "By the way don't forget Phillip Greenaway's strap line, as sponsor, he'll want his pound of flesh, come to think of it this will be the closest he's ever come to actually buying anyone a drink!"

"The advertising posters will say, "Sponsored by Greenaway's Estate Agent, Find your Perfect Match then see us to find your perfect Love Nest" It's tacky and ridiculous so absolutely Phillip to a tee!" Jamie laughed as he looked at the poster.

Drew put his pad down and sipped his dry sherry. "Phillip will be here trying to pick up any left-over crumpet so we may need to warn the punters! Right, that's sorted then, all we need now, is a stopwatch, name badges and the forms for the daters to complete." Drew was finishing his drink when Blair and Bridget wandered in.

"Can't stop for another, I'm off to see Miss Stuffy Knickers about her wardrobe, it was the only way I could get her to agree to join in." Drew grabbed his astrakhan coat and shoulder bag and departed in his usual dramatic style.

In her room at The Malmsbury Spa Miranda sifted through the limited selection in her wardrobe and felt totally deflated; she had not bought anything new for years, most of her clothing allowance went on tailored trouser suits because she spent the majority of her time working. A shy girl, Miranda had struggled to attract the opposite sex mainly due to the fact that she dressed quite conservatively and clammed up every time they tried to engage her in conversation; she had also spent most of her time forging her career. A knock at the door announced the arrival of Drew who immediately got started.

"It looks like I might have my work cut out here, but I love a challenge so let's see what we can do." He began removing items from her wardrobe. "No, no, definitely not. I don't know why you won't let me take you shopping." Drew moved the hangers noisily along the rail. "This can't be all you own; my sweater collection alone would fill this wardrobe."

"I come out in hives if I even as much as look at a dress." Miranda looked despondently at her choices.

Drew continued searching in earnest, stooping to pick up an article that had fallen to the floor. "Now, this I might be able to do something with." He pulled out a stone coloured shift dress with kick pleat and sleeves. "If I remove that in favour of a standard split and take off the caps over the arms, this could be just what we're looking for."

"Go ahead," said Miranda looking at the crumpled dress, "it's not been worn in years so do whatever you think best."

"Well I'm pretty handy on the machine but if I get stuck I'll call Dolly Masters – and book yourself into 'Wax Lyrical' to get your hair and nails done, this might well be your coming out party! In fact why not go the whole hog get a wax and vagazil while you're about it." Drew took one look at Miranda's dumbfounded look and knew it was going to be an uphill struggle.

"On second thoughts, stick to what you're comfortable with, a hairdo and manicure and I'll pop this dress round when it's done."

On the evening of the 24th, following much coercion the speed dating victims began to assemble in Hendersons. Jamie was relieved to see that there was a good crowd in who were simply there to gawp and nosy but it meant that the daters didn't feel quite so conspicuous. Luke had added a caveat to the poster campaign stating that half the proceeds of the event would go to 'Help the Heroes'. As a former soldier it was a charity close to his heart. Olivia, reading the poster, whilst waiting at the bar for her free drink couldn't help but feel that being on the lookout for love was actually a selfless act on her part as she was also contributing to a worthy cause, began to relax and look forward to the evening ahead.

Drew was attending to last minute details and generally bustling about when he felt a tap on his shoulder. Spinning around, he nearly fell over at the sight before him. Miranda stood, a vision of sophisticated elegance, although clearly a little self-conscious, totally transformed. Her hair, normally scraped neatly back in a ponytail, was now softly layered and tousled with curls. Her makeup was expertly applied; Miranda having followed Drew's instructions and spent the afternoon being pampered at 'Wax Lyrical Beauty Parlour' on the High Street. Finally the simple, beige shift dress now adorned with mocha accessories, that Drew had amazingly salvaged, showed off her previously concealed curvy figure to perfection.

"Oh! My! God!" Drew exclaimed loudly, shocking those around him. "Your light has most definitely been hidden under one huge, fat bushel for far too long girlfriend," he squealed at Miranda becoming more like Louie Spence the more excited he became. Drew linked arms with the now blushing Miranda and headed to the bar for a fortifying drink and to show off his creation to Blair and the other girls.

Elizabeth Montgomery enjoyed the distinguished companionship provided by her evenings spent with Major Ronaldson. After several months of attending mainly social functions together she had recently accepted a dinner invitation and for the first time she had managed to address him by name, Horatio, instead of by title as she normally did, and this had felt a strangely intimate moment for someone so reserved. So this particular Friday evening found the Major and Elizabeth having pre-dinner drinks in Hendersons wine bar.

Returning from powdering her nose Elizabeth was somewhat surprised to find another female sitting across from her companion and avidly engaging in conversation.

"So do you come here often?" the stranger was asking the Major.

"Well quite frequently yes," spluttered the Major totally confused and desperately trying to signal to Elizabeth who was standing behind the interloper.

"Well I'm Deborah, I work in accounts. You don't seem to have a tag on?" The interloper continued.

The Major looking like a goldfish with his mouth wide open managed to respond,

"Madam, do I know you?"

"None of us know each other, dear, that's the whole point of it. Just a five minute quickie is all you get to make up your mind." As she said this Elizabeth had moved forward to reclaim her seat.

"I beg your pardon?" She exploded and turning on her heel she marched over to the bar where Jamie was busy serving a long line of customers.

"Jamie Henderson what sort of establishment are you running here? Poor Major Ronaldson has just been propositioned by a lady of the night!" Elizabeth elbowed the waiting customers out of the way to get to the bar and it was Jamie's turn to be bemused. He looked over in the direction of the Major who had by now turned puce with discomfort and he quickly assessed the situation.

"No problem here Elizabeth, I think one of our speed daters has accidentally joined your table, I'll come over and sort it out." He chuckled to himself, thinking this could only happen to Elizabeth and the Major.

A very flustered Elizabeth returned to the table with Jamie by her side where the Major was now deep in conversation with Deborah "from accounts."

"How very disappointing," she remarked when Jamie explained her mistake, "the good ones are always taken." She added to Elizabeth who was irritated to see the Major blush with pride.

When the queue of customers finally eased off Jamie surveyed the crowded room and was pleased to see the bar was busy not just with regulars, who he was of course grateful to see, but also new faces drawn in by the evening's themed event. In this current economic climate he was well aware that socialising would probably be one of the luxuries that people would curtail and neither he nor Luke were prepared to give up the comfortable lifestyle. Therefore a little extra effort was going to be needed to encourage the punters to come in and spend money. Hard work didn't daunt him though, in fact he thrived on it.

Drew rang the old brass bell on the bar, usually reserved for last orders and fire drills, to attract the attention of the daters.

"Ladies and gentlemen, we are about to begin tonight's Speed Date event. You should all be in possession of a badge with either the letter A or B on it." With an exaggerated flourish he held up a paper badge to illustrate his meaning. "If you are wearing an 'a' please take a seat at one of the designated tables; if you are a 'b' please wait for me to ring the bell again and then go to a vacant position opposite a seated 'a' person. Are we all clear?" He looked over his half rimmed spectacles and surveyed the confusion.

"Every five minutes I'll ding-a-ling and I am only talking to the 'bs' now," general tittering responded to this remark, "you must move one space left. Do we all know what we are doing? You're under starters orders!" Again he surveyed the sea of blank faces in front of him and turned to Jamie behind the bar, "Pour me another Babycham, it's going to be a long night with this lot!!!" And with that he energetically rang the bell and the event was underway.

Olivia was feeling distinctly sceptical about the evening. She had succumbed to pressure from Bridget and agreed to up the numbers largely by way of supporting Jamie and Luke who in the past had helped out with a couple of sticky moments at the hotel. To show her general lack of enthusiasm for the event she had deliberately dressed down and had arrived early with Bridget to ensure she'd had a couple of bracing shots of The Introduction cocktail to steady her nerves. She was now sat opposite Tristram, who was in his early fifties, trim and well turned out. He owned a considerable amount of land in the area and in days gone by he would have been the country squire. Olivia had met Tristram at many hotel social events and felt decidedly uncomfortable about being interviewed by him as a possible romantic attachment which was to her mind, frankly preposterous. To his credit Tristram looked equally ill at ease and immediately broke the ice.

"Nice to see you Olivia, I assume you're doing this to support Jamie and Luke rather than to find true love, not unlike myself?" He picked up his gin and tonic and downed it in one.

"Well yes I am actually, Tristram," she answered

truthfully. "I already know most of the people here so it is unlikely cupid's going to strike tonight."

"Right then," he responded enthusiastically, "might as well talk shop while we've got a minute. I've been put in charge of organising the Gloucestershire Countryside Alliance meeting at Easter, I was going to call you to see about booking the Malmsbury."

Olivia relaxed and laughed as got her diary out of her bag, at least the evening wouldn't be a total waste if she got a good booking for the hotel out of it. Jamie, watching from the bar, was slightly concerned to see Olivia, whom he'd always been quite keen on, booking a date in her diary with Tristram who was almost old enough to be her father. In order to break things up he grabbed the bell from off the bar next to Drew, who was too busy gawping at the daters to notice, and rang it like mad. He hoped that would scupper any plans Tristram might have had.

On the far side of the room Matthew Jenkins was sitting uncomfortably in his number 12 spot waiting for the next gargoyle to inflict her five minutes of pained conversation on him. He'd only agreed to come because his older brother Simon wanted to have a crack at Alicia the busty barmaid, but Matthew didn't think he stood a chance, Alicia only had eyes for Luke. Matthew had had one promising moment earlier when he'd spent an interesting few minutes with Pippa Hamilton. Pippa ran the Flipping Bodbury area Pony Club, with a pretty face and voluptuous figure, no doubt from all that bouncing in the saddle, she wan an attractive proposition but painfully unsure of herself and so self-conscious Matthew wasn't sure he could be bothered to pursue her. As a third year medical student he was doing a three month rotation at the town's health centre shadowing one of the GPs so he'd had an opportunity to check out the local talent. Just as he was about to be descended upon by a large, blonde woman spilling out of a pink chiffon blouse with hoop earrings that were dragging her lobes down to her shoulders, he noticed a rather tipsy Bridgett stumble into the table by the exit and decided to rush to the aid of a damsel in distress rather than face the drag queen who was bearing down on him.

Miranda's nerves got the better of her during the first two five-minute sessions. Her first prospective date had been a middle aged gentleman named Fraser who worked as a driver for the local abattoir and try as she might Miranda had failed to engage in any light-hearted banter with him whilst the vision of cattle on their way to slaughter kept appearing in her head. The second encounter introduced her to Shane, a lad of perhaps middle twenties who she felt was probably there as a bet and seemed to only have one subject to talk about, namely himself and his attempts to become a radio DJ, he was intent on getting Miranda to book him for discos at the hotel to give him more experience. By the fourth session she had finished a second glass of wine, she was stridently avoiding the lethal cocktail Luke was promoting, and was beginning to relax a bit. The initial discomfort of wearing a dress was slowly beginning to wear off and the reality that everyone in the room was treating the evening in a light-hearted manner rather than a route to true romance, allowed her to start chatting more freely and enjoy the experience. When the bell rang for the fifth session Miranda found herself sitting opposite Kieran Sadler. Although they had never formerly met Miranda had seen Kieran around town and was immediately impressed by his smart but casual appearance and his welcoming smile as she took her seat opposite him. After the formal introductions were out of the way Miranda found Kieran easy to chat to and found he had a surprisingly good sense of humour. Kieran too was beginning to think the evening wasn't such a waste of time. Having been press-ganged into it by Jamie and Luke to boost the male numbers he now found Miranda was easy on the eye and charming company. The bell rang out from the bar announcing the five minutes were up and Drew addressed the speed daters atop a bar stool.

"Ladies and Gentlemen, we shall be taking the first of our interval breaks. Please help yourselves to my nibbles." This caused general tittering as he no doubt intended it too. "And of course there are refills of this evenings special cocktail The Introduction, lined up on the bar to help wet your whistle for more conversation to follow." Drew unsteadily dismounted, clipboard in hand and began to move about the room assessing the progress of the evening so far.

"Can I get you a drink Miranda?" Kieran immediately asked in order to ensure she didn't dash off to talk to someone else.

"Yes please, but just a soft drink, I think I need to pace myself." She pointed in Bridget's direction who was swaying unsteadily at the bar chatting to Jamie and Luke. Kieran went off to the bar and Bridget spying Miranda tottered over to her.

"What gives with the lovely Kieran?" Bridget untactfully asked; subtlety was never her strong point.

"He's very nice pleasant company. He's just getting me a drink." Miranda replied smiling at her friend knowing full well she expected more of an answer than that.

"Well, I'll just push off then and leave you to it." Bridget smiled back, "I've had a bit of luck myself. No 12 rescued me when I had a little trip he's going to be a doctor! I need to see if Livvie has been lucky in love too." She wandered away concentrating steadfastly on placing her feet one in front of the other as Olivia came towards her with a plate of food no doubt with the intention of soaking up some of the alcohol Bridget had downed.

The interval time passed quickly with Miranda and Kieran chatting easily and she was reluctant to leave such good company to return to meeting the next prospective date.

"You must really enjoy the challenge in your line of work?" Miranda was saying, "I mean I love the hotel industry because I get to meet new people all the time but it must be a thrilling experience saving animals and delivering new life." She realised as soon as she'd said it that she sounded like a gushing teenager but Kieran showed no sign of being uncomfortable.

"It's a fantastically rewarding job but it does have its downsides. It's hard not being able to save every animal you treat, the animal cruelty you see and of course being on call is very anti-social." The moment he said this, his pager bleeped.

"Sorry Miranda, I must just make a quick call and see if I'm needed." He grabbed his mobile out of his pocket.

"Of course," she responded, hiding her disappointment.

Whilst Kieran left the room Miranda looked around at her fellow speed daters and felt somewhat deflated that she had to continue with the next session in just a few minutes. Kieran quickly returned to her side.

"I'm afraid I've got to go. There's a goat in labour and the kid is stuck so I'm needed. It shouldn't be too much of a problem but I have to get over to Haslow's farm." He began to put his jacket on.

"I understand, I hope everything goes well," she responded truthfully.

"Look I know this is a bit unusual, but if you aren't desperate to stay here why not come with me and see what I do for yourself, only if you're interested of course?" He looked embarrassed but Miranda didn't need to be asked twice.

"I'll just grab my coat and be right with you." She eagerly accepted as Drew announced the next five minute session was about to start. Bridget, now ensconced at the bar with Matthew and Blair, all drinking lemonade to keep clear heads, noticed the two departing figures dashing out of the room and got completely the wrong idea.

"That Miranda's a real dark horse!" she said to Drew who forgot to ring the bell to start the daters again as he was also staring open-mouthed at the exit.

"Just goes to show what a bit of good haute couture can do! Now come on Bridget, this delightful young man is waiting to treat you to a bar meal." He gave her a friendly nudge in Matthew's direction and they headed round to the dining area. Drew ticked them off his clipboard lift, he was keeping note of how many matches he had managed to instigate!

"I think we might just make this a regular event," he said to Blair, "I'm obviously turning out to be a proper little Cupid!"